Girls Weekend

C.M. Nascosta

a MonsterBait romance

xoxo
CM Nascosta

Girls Weekend

C.M. Nascosta

a MonsterBait romance

cmnascosta.com

Original Title
Girls Weekend

Design, Illustration and Cover Art
Ilustrariane

Text revision
C.M. Nascosta

ISBN
978-1-7365466-0-4
Meduas Editoriale

To all my Monster Bait thirst trappers: thank you for all of your boundless support and humor, and for being as invested in these characters as I am. Stay thirsty! Much gratitude to Irym for being an unwitting guiding light on this story's path. Thank you to Ariane, for being the best partner a dumb writer could ask for; and to Michelle, for always being my Annie Wilkes.

C.M. Nascosta

Part 01

♥ *The Arrival* ♥

The small hamlet was tucked into a sun-washed valley, surrounded by rolling green hills. The drive from Cambric Creek was short and easy: a straight shot up a country road, nothing but fields dotted with cows and corn the whole way.

"I want to get some fresh-pressed cider," Silva piped up cheerfully from the backseat. "And hopefully, we can find a cute little bistro for dinner tonight!"

Lurielle kept her gaze trained out the window, not daring to turn in Ris's direction, knowing the smile on her friend's face would be evil. Silva was new to their friend circle, only having started at the office a few months earlier. Girl-next-door pretty, in pastel twinsets and twee dresses, she was the exact type of elf to

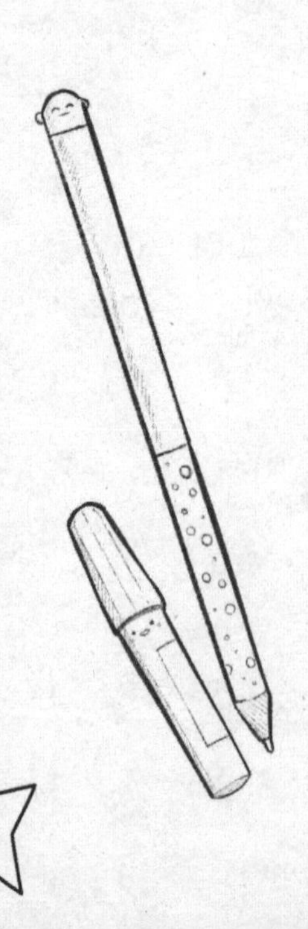

whom Lurielle had been frequently compared when she had been an awkward, chubby teenager. Slender and shapely, Silva's chestnut-colored hair was shiny and smooth, her skin an even, flawless lavender, her green eyes wide and guileless. Lurielle had tried hard to hate her on principle, but Silva was also unfailingly sweet and good-natured, friendly to everyone, and impossible to dislike.

When Ris had made the plans for the trip, it had been guilt-wrenching not to tell Silva. She was there every day, bringing in homemade cookies and making coffee for everyone, joining the girls for lunches in the break room, and cheerfully calling out goodbyes at the end of each day.

"She's going to feel bad!" Lurielle had hissed as she and Ris hovered over the human resource department's copy machine several weeks prior, popping her head up periodically to scan the room for their cheerful co-worker. "When she finds out we all went on a trip without her, she's going to feel terrible!"

"Do you honestly think little Miss Sunshine wants to be on her knees all weekend? It's hard to avoid grass stains when you're being spit-roasted, you know. Those are her debutante pearls. Aren't you going to feel bad when she clutches them so hard the strand breaks?"

Lurielle had snorted, envisioning the flawless pearls gracing Silva's slim neck. "You know, when you put it that way, I'm not sure *I* want to be spit-roasted all weekend either."

"Of course you do," Ris assured decisively. "We both do. That's the point! The men around here are trash, dating is a punishment, and we want to get laid. We'll have to come back to our humdrum lives on Monday, but at least the three days of orgasms will give us something to smile over. Just don't say anything about it! It's not like it's appropriate to talk about at work anyways. Do I need to send you to a workshop?"

Lurielle just glared. "You're the one who works in HR talking about being spit-roasted, but *I'm* the one who needs a workshop?"

When Dynah backed out a few days before the trip, citing her hope that the Dragonborn guy she'd just met on an interspecies dating app might be *the one*, Ris's plan to keep Silva in the dark changed, to keep the cost of the weekend evenly split three ways. Their wide-eyed co-worker was thrilled to be included in the girls' trip on their long weekend off from work, and had arrived at Lurielle's on Friday afternoon, a butter-yellow scarf expertly knotted at her throat and her quilted, floral-print weekender in tow. She was, as far as Lurielle knew, entirely oblivious to the nature of the weekend trip.

There had been many jokes about visiting the commune, suppositions over the endowments possessed by the burly residents, squealing assertions that once they'd arrived, they might never come home. Lurielle had never anticipated they'd ever follow through with it someday. Yet here she was, she thought, eyeing the roadside sign announcing the hamlet just ahead, riding shotgun in Ris's car, their bags packed with little more than skimpy bathing suits, a few sundresses, and backup birth control; sweet, innocent Silva in tow.

There was a glittering lake to the side of the road ahead, and Silva oohed over how picturesque it looked, remarking that maybe there

were paddle boats. As the car approached, the girls could see brawny, forest-green shoulders rising from the sparkling surface, muscular arms making long strokes to the lake's edge, close to the road. Lurielle straightened at the sight, biting her lip in anticipation.

The immense body emerging from the surface rippled with well-defined muscle; long, jet-black hair braided down his back. Droplets sparkled from his shoulders, and his considerable endowment stood at half-mast, bobbing as he flipped his wet hair back. Lurielle pressed her thighs together in excitement. *This* was what they'd come for. A massive hand wrapped around the stiffened length as the car neared, giving it a slow pump before the orc raised his head at the sound of the approaching car of wide-eyed elves. The girls watched in silence as the huge orc released his partial erection, raising the same hand with a lazy smile as they passed. Lurielle could hear Silva breathing hard in the backseat, her lavender nose pressed to the window.

"Ladies," Ris announced confidently, turning the wheel to direct the car into the hamlet's road, "this is going to be the *best* weekend."

♥♥♥

"Where do you think we should go first?"

Ris held a skimpy mesh poncho up to her long body, the beaded fringe on the bottom hem hitting her plum-colored thighs. The magenta scrap of fabric was meant to be a swimsuit cover-up, but Lurielle knew her friend was contemplating wearing the crisscrossing silken strands on their own.

"I think," she said carefully, watching Ris pull a transparent gossamer wrap from her bag, "that you should put on a normal dress, something that at least covers your nipples, and we'll go to dinner. Let's scope the place out a little before walking into a club dressed like we're looking for a gang bang."

"But that *is* what I'm looking for!" The tall elf grinned wickedly in the mirror at Lurielle, who rolled her eyes, turning away with a click of her tongue.

"You're worse than a man. Just put some real clothes on and let's head out, okay? We can look for some extracurriculars after dinner, and if Silva doesn't want to come, she can go back to the room."

She found Silva gripping the drapery in the common room of their rented suite, her eyes fixed on something out the window as her teeth worried her lower lip. As she approached, she was able to see the object of Silva's attention: the well-rounded backside of the orc kneeling in the grass just ahead, gathering up what appeared to be a set of lawn darts. There were dimples above the delectable swell of his ass, and Lurielle thought she could see a spray of sage-colored freckles across his broad, hunter green shoulders. Silva's bulging eyes found Lurielle's then, her voice taking a moment longer to catch up with her moving jaw.

"Wha-what kind of place is this?" she asked in a hushed whisper, slim eyebrows knitting together as she glanced out the window again.

Lurielle idly thought she should start keeping track of her sighs that weekend. "It's a nudist commune," she admitted, avoiding Silva's

eye. "Why don't you get ready for dinner? We'll try to find a little bistro like you—"

"But why? Why did we come to a nudist town? Are we going to be *naked* all weekend?!"

If we're lucky! Lurielle thought, fighting to keep a neutral face.

"We don't need to be. It's just the guys who live here, for the most part."

"But why—"

"Because they're hot orcs, Silv. Hot, sexy, *naked* orcs." *Naked and horny,* she thought, keeping that part of the description to herself. The orcs in this particular village were well-known to have tremendous libidos. It was a common knowledge rumor that they satisfied their appetites without restraint with the regular stream of tourists from neighboring towns who visited to *sightsee*.

"Naked and horny," Ris announced, entering the room in a gossamer pink wrap dress that at least covered her nipples, Lurielle noted in relief. "We're here to get laid, Silva. I haven't been on a single good date in almost a year, and the best lay I've had was that minotaur we met at that trivia bar. Lurielle's been living like a nun since she and Tev split up. You don't have to do anything you don't want to; you're free to keep your panties on all weekend. But at least enjoy the sights! You're never going to get to see this much uncovered cock anywhere at home! But *I'm* not going home without sampling the local goods, preferably buffet-style. Now go change so we can get dinner."

She almost felt sorry as Silva struggled in place for a moment, attempting to move her feet towards the bedroom but unable to tear her eyes away from the orc ass out the window. When at last the bedroom door closed behind her, Lurielle turned to Ris with a shrug. "Hopefully, they have paddle boats. She can spend the weekend in the middle of the lake being appalled with us."

"That's fine," Ris laughed. "As long as I go home bow-legged, I don't care. At least she'll go home with a story to tell, right?"

♥♥♥

Are you sure you want to wear that?

Her mother's voice piped up as she turned in the mirror, eyeing the way her two-piece's bottom stretched over an ass that certainly wasn't the same size as it had been in undergrad. *You should probably skip dessert, babe.* Between her ex and her mother, Lurielle never felt alone in her head, always hearing one of the other two voices who occupied the tight space, reminding her of her deficits.

Grimacing in the mirror, she looked over the soft swell of her stomach, the wide set of her hips, the full breasts that sagged a bit too much to look good naked. *What were you thinking coming here? You look like a snowman.* She was positive the overhead lighting was designed to make her flaws stand out. Her fair skin had been described as "peaches and cream" by an aesthetician at the salon she'd visited shortly after her move to Cambric Creek, but the sallow reflection in the mirror lacked a peach's warm blush. She'd had honeyed highlights

put in, brightening her dull blonde waves, had given the stylist—an intimidatingly glamorous hulder with expertly winged eyeliner—free rein to cut it any way she wanted. Lurielle had gone as long as she could without washing her hair after the salon appointment, dreading the moment the soft, smooth waves would fall out, knowing she'd never be able to replicate the style at home. All she saw now, in the mirror's harsh lighting, was uncooperative hair, indistinct hazel eyes, and a spray of freckles over her pug-like nose. She was dumpy next to Ris, didn't possess Silva's polished sparkle, would be ignored by the men here, all used to beautiful, leggy tourists...*stop it! You're here to have fun, not feel sorry for yourself all weekend.*

Since moving to Cambric Creek for a job, she'd done her damnedest to overcome her insecurities and bad habits, quashing the voices in her head the best she could, despite the way they'd taken hold in her mind like an invasive vine. She'd developed better-eating habits, had made new friends, and bought a wardrobe that flattered her shape. She'd joined an aerobic dance class that made her feel foolish and sweat to a truly horrifying degree, but she found other women there like her: curvy goblins looking to lose baby weight and wide-hipped werecats, eager to rid themselves of the padding they'd gained at university. They were all as uncoordinated and ungainly as her, making the weekly experience fun, rather than yet another exercise in self-torture.

None of that seemed to matter just then, as she prepared to head down to the party deck hot tubs in a two-piece next to her tall, willowy friend. *You can do this,* Lurielle encouraged herself, wrapping a gauzy blue pareo around her neck, knotted at her hip. *It's already dark out, you can get in the water, and no one will see you. They'll all be drooling over Ris anyways.*

Silva had gasped in relief earlier when their handsome server at the small restaurant was fully clothed; his dark hair casually pulled into a loose bun. He'd grinned knowingly when Ris had pointedly asked where they could partake of the *local attractions*. The fountain garden, the nightclub, the sauna at the resort spa...he'd ticked off the best "tourist spots" on long, slender fingers in a lightly accented voice, advising them to visit the poolside bar that night to get a feel for the crowd, adding that he himself frequented the little bar on the corner. The light from the pendant lamp above the small table shone on the silver bands around his tusks as he winked before leaving to put their order in, and Silva flushed until she was nearly as dark as Ris.

Now they were taking his advice, heading to the poolside tiki bar, leaving Silva behind at her request. The thumping bass of loud music seemed to vibrate the walls as soon as the girls entered the corridor leading to the deck, the noise frequently broken up by a chorus of loud, masculine laughter. Lurielle realized she didn't need to worry about being gawked at, her physical flaws on display for this group of strangers, for the packed press of bodies didn't allow for contemplation of anyone's form.

There were at least two dozen orcs filling up the tight space, all of them clothed, and Ris exclaimed in disappointment. Their cute server

had let it slip that anywhere money was changing hands for alcohol, clothing was required. Lurielle had a feeling that meant Silva would be spending the weekend perched at the end of a bar, demurely sipping Shirley Temples and clutching her handbag.

"I'm getting one of them into the pool with me," Ris exclaimed, a determined look in her eyes. "Ugh, there are so many tourists here!"

"Isn't that what we are?" Lurielle wasn't sure what she'd been expecting from the resort, but this over-crowded meat market hadn't been it. In addition to the abundance of burly orcs, giggling women and overconfident men of varying species packed into the bar and small dance floor, and groping hands seemed to be everywhere. The girls had barely taken a few steps before a hyena-faced man with a cocky smile slid his arm around Lurielle's waist, asking if she wanted a drink. The music was overloud, the flashing lights too bright, and she winced at the sharp cackle coming from a skimpily dressed harpy, drink sloshing as the girl stumbled on the dancefloor.

"Sure, why not?" she choked out with an uneasy laugh, gripping Ris's hand and pulling her along. *You're going to make the best of it.* "We'll both have Cosmos."

♥♥♥

The sounds of music and hooting laughter spilled from the small bar out to the sidewalk where Silva stood, chewing her lip indecisively. Every few minutes, the *chink!* of a pool cue could be heard glinting off the side of a polished ball inside the bar. *They'll all have their clothes on*, she reminded herself, squaring her slim shoulders in resolve. Dive bars were not the sort of establishments she normally patronized at home, but...*but you're on vacation. There's no one around to judge. Stop being ridiculous, you know how to do this.* With the impressive stick up her gym-toned ass, daytime Silva was sometimes, unfortunately, a challenging skin to shed.

She'd been thrilled when Ris and Lurielle had invited her to come this weekend. Her co-workers *were* all very nice, had been welcoming and friendly when she'd started in the office earlier in the year, but sometimes it was hard not to feel like she existed on the periphery of firmly established friend groups.

It was hard, she thought privately, to be an elf in Cambric Creek. She knew her co-workers found the Elvish community snobbish; the whole town did. She'd wondered as an adolescent why her forebears had even settled there, choosing to make the multispecies community their home, realizing as she grew older that it had been the hubris of simply expecting to be welcome everywhere they went. What her goblin and gnomish and werecat co-workers didn't understand was the likely reality that she'd be attending, not just their own funerals someday, but their children's and grandchildren's. Elves weren't immortal, too much inbreeding with humans and other lesser species over the years for that,

but they were much longer lived than the vast majority of their peers. It was natural that they kept to themselves as a result, she thought.

To have been included in the trip with her Elvish co-workers was a big step, she'd thought. *If you hide in the room the whole weekend, you'll never be asked to do anything again!* She couldn't help it. The thought of going down to the crowded deck bar, pressed between groping hands and hulking, naked bodies was slightly terrifying, completely uncouth, and not something in which an elf of good breeding would be interested.

It wasn't that she was uninterested in *meeting* someone, far from it. Goddess knew she dated, what with her grandmother keeping close tabs on her social life, poking and prodding and carrying on about wanting to see her beneath the binding tree before she died, but *this*... this wasn't about finding a boyfriend. This was voyeurism, indulging in a carelessly anonymous fling at best, and the thought of being surrounded by huge, naked men all weekend, even if the sight of them was exciting, was overwhelming.

The young orc from the restaurant had seemed different, though, less imposing than the others she'd seen so far, which was why she now stood on the sidewalk, waffling. Tate, he'd called himself as he took their drink order, a simple, compact name that lacked the guttural harshness she'd come to expect from the Orcish language. Compared to the hulking brute who had erupted from the tranquil lake that morning as their car had passed, Tate had seemed slender and short for an orc, with a laughing glint in his eyes and an appealing air of mischief about him. When he'd winked at her, after pointedly telling their table he would be at the little dive bar on the corner once he got off work, she'd felt heat spread to the tips of her long, slender ears. *You probably looked like a blueberry.*

After Lurielle and Ris had headed to the tiki bar without her, she'd spent close to thirty minutes pacing the small rented room before aggravation had pushed her outside. She'd gone wandering, irritated with herself for being such an uptight little mouse. She'd been *fun* once; Silva was sure of it. She knew she was fortunate to have found her first real job out of school right in her hometown. When she'd expressed a desire to go to art school, her mother and grandmother had formed a united front in their persuasion to keep her on the path they'd laid out for her—a path which contained no stop at the small, liberal fine arts school in which she'd expressed interest.

"Darling, you won't be able to pledge to Ilma in a place like that, and it would break our hearts if you didn't have that foundation once you're off on your own!" The compromise had been a school several hours away from home, primarily Elvish and full of good families with eligible sons, but still far enough away that she'd been able to breathe for the first time in her life. Now though...the freedom of university—the parties and late nights, frat house mixers and weekend hookups, a life away from Cambric Creek and her grandmother's prying eyes, and the daily weight of *expectation*—seemed like a lifetime ago.

She'd been deep in thought when she'd passed the bistro again.

"You look lost, little dove." He'd been leaning on the brick wall outside the entrance, the glow from the end of his cigarette a bright

flare in the twilight. The lopsided smirk he gave her had an odd glint to it, but there was something about the shape of his face—high cheekbones and a narrow nose, much finer than the other orcs she'd seen that day—that somewhat set her at ease.

"Not lost," she'd laughed hesitantly. "Just...deciding."

His smirk had widened to a grin, and Silva couldn't be certain in the dying light, but there seemed to be too many teeth in his mouth, gleaming sharp, a slightly sinister effect she didn't remember him possessing in the bistro's golden lighting. Even so, as he raised the cigarette to his lips once more, taking a deep drag, she stepped closer, feeling her ears burn at the doe-eyed look she knew she was giving him. *You're as bad as a human, always falling for the bad boy.*

"Well, if you're looking for the *sights*," he'd paused, raising a slim black brow meaningfully, "you'll want to head up to the pool, or else back down the way you came, to the cabins."

She wasn't sure what sort of face she'd pulled, for she'd been treated to even more teeth as his smile widened further. His skin was a pale lichen green, and three slim, silver loops glimmered in his arched black brow, matching the line of rings that curved up his long ear. The lilt in his voice was what her grandmother would have termed "from the old country," an indication that the place he called home was far across the sea. Although he seemed smaller than the other orcs she'd seen, he'd towered over her in the dim glow of the streetlamp, long and leanly muscled, and she'd been breathless as he'd leaned down to murmur conspiratorially in her ear.

"If you're looking for a different kind of crowd, the south end of town here is where you'll want to stay. That's where I'll be," he'd gestured with the cigarette to a creaking sign on the side of an old building, just down the block, "at the Pixie...drinks on me if you *decide* to stop in, dove. I hope you do."

She stood beneath the sign now, *The Plundered Pixie*, giving it a proper look over now that she wasn't squinting up the block. The creaking iron featured the silhouette of the titular pixie; her wings outstretched as she was...Silva blushed when she realized that the shape behind the pixie was a satyr, their forms locked together, giving the bar's name meaning. *No more waffling*, she decided resolutely, hearing the sounds of laughter approaching up the sidewalk. The longer she loitered on the street, the more likely she was to be accosted by one of the nudists. She would be, wonder of wonders, safer in the little pub. *Time to decide...*

Pulling the door open with bated breath, the sight of bar patrons had her exhaling in short-lived relief. Big and brawny and completely clothed, wearing jeans and tight t-shirts, leather vests and enormous belt buckles, pierced and tattooed. Even hunched over pool tables, the orcs seemed massive to her, and several sets of eyes moved over her appraisingly as she crossed the threshold, feeling on display and out of place. *This was a bad idea.* The pub itself was larger than she'd expected, with high ceilings of beamed lumber and amber-hued lighting. As her eyes swept the room, she spotted an empty stool on the far side of the bar, tucked out of the

way where she'd be able to keep her head down and go unnoticed by anyone, sip a cocktail or two before going back to the room like the pathetic little mouse she was—

"I'm glad you took my advice, dove." The lilting brogue in her ear was comfortingly familiar, the tension in her narrow shoulders dropping ever-so-slightly at his voice.

His mischief-filled eyes were the color of late-autumn honey, and his smile was wider than she thought it should be, but Silva was relieved all the same.

"Hi," she murmured breathlessly, turning in relief.

Tate had been the only orc on the floor in the small bistro earlier that evening, but now, amidst a room full of others, Silva could see that her initial suppositions were accurate: he was far smaller in stature than the other orcs in the room, lean and lithe, his slender tusks only extending a bit past his upper lip and ending in sharp points. His hair was still up in a messy bun, pulled back from his delicate-looking face, but he'd changed, the white button-down and black pants of his uniform having been swapped for a fitted black tee and snug, battered jeans. His high cheekbones and long jaw gave him a vaguely aristocratic air, his limbs were long and graceful, and his unusual eyes sparkled with an unnatural brightness. He was ridiculously handsome, she thought. *Even Nana would think so! Just relax and enjoy yourself for a change.*

"Drink?" he asked, steering her through the crowd with a hand at her waist. Directing her to the far end of the bar, he called out to the bartender in Orcish. Silva felt a quiver of nervous excitement move up her back as the massive orc nodded, setting a golden-hued glass before her a moment later. "It's similar to Mirúlvin, so don't drink it too fast," Tate advised with another sharp-edged smile when a second glass was slid to where he stood beside her bar stool.

Silva looked up in surprise. "How do you know about—"

Cutting herself off, she gave the handsome orc another once over. Mirúlvin—a fortified Elvish wine made from fermented sweet berries—was deceptively strong, a lesson every young elf learned the hard way at some point in their adolescence. Silva couldn't imagine why an orc would know such a thing, not unless..."You're not *just* an orc."

The roman baths were a long hall of echoing marble, the air thick with steam from the roiling pools of water, and every step she took reverberated between the columns, the sound trapped and rattling in the heavy vapor. The room was empty, save for the massive upper back of the orc reclining in the far left marble tub. Lurielle paused, realizing she was well away from the relative safety of the bar, and the orc before her was bound to be unclothed.

She'd left Ris on the party deck, where the tall elf was attempting to cajole not one but two brawny orcs into stripping down and joining her in the hot tubs. Lurielle had cut herself off after three drinks, wanting to remember anything humiliating she might do and not entirely trusting of the wandering hands of some of the other resort guests. The groping hands, thumping music, and copious alcohol were giving her a headache, reminding her of every sorority party and late night club at which she'd felt uncomfortable in undergrad. Deciding to leave early and join Silva, she'd passed the sign pointing towards the roman baths, choosing to make a quick detour to check out the space.

"Plenty of room in here, darlin'." The orc's voice rose from the steam, a deep, unexpected drawl that made Lurielle shiver, despite the heat. His voice was that of a stranger's, but as she stepped closer, he turned, giving her a lazy smile that she recognized instantly.

It was the orc from the lake that morning, his long black braid disappearing behind him, his massive, well-muscled arms stretched out across the marble back of the tub. "Water's nice and hot. Very relaxin'...you're not going to want to get that pretty dress wet, though."

His voice was like a sweet syrup, thick and dark and slow-moving, and Lurielle couldn't explain the trance it seemed to put her in, why it relaxed her at the same time it quickened her breath, but she drew ever closer to the steaming water as if pulled by his drawling cadence. The blue pareo was a tangle of fabric, and it took her several fumbling moments to locate the knot, undone with trembling fingers. She tugged the gauzy heap free, feeling gooseflesh rise on her skin as she turned hesitantly to the water, gripping the hand railing convulsively.

The orc before her was devastatingly handsome, with a large, square jaw and dimpled chin. His nose was long and straight, and thick black brows arched over heavily-hooded eyes, matching his lazy smile and syrupy drawl. His luxurious-looking hair formed a sharp widow's peak at his brow, with several slim lines of beaded braiding over one of his pointed ears. Lurielle felt his eyes dragging over her as she slowly stepped into the steaming water, her heart climbing into her throat. Surely he was used to svelte elves, like Ris; to lithe werecats and leanly muscled orc women. Her dimpled thighs and muffin top were far from impressive, far from impressive, in comparison. Hesitating, she wondered if she'd be able to escape from the steamy room without making an even bigger fool of herself. She wasn't able to force herself to look up until she was concealed in the water up to her waist, and was surprised to find his full lips curled up in a smile.

"Careful now, not too fast. It's hot, you wanna give yourself a chance to adjust."

She wondered, feeling a rush of adrenaline melt away a bit of her self-consciousness as the steam rose around her, if his words were a way to prolong looking at her.

"What brings a pretty little thing like you over this way tonight?" he asked once she'd settled into the water, seated across from him. "All alone?"

"Oh, um...I-I'm here with some friends...we were at the tiki bar on the deck for a bit, but that's not really my scene."

"Oh, no, ma'am. Too noisy for me. I come here to relax, not to go to bed with a migraine."

Lurielle smiled at his words, not expecting the sentiment, nor believing that the handsome orc went to bed alone very often. "Do-do you not live here?"

"I have a membership to the resort club," he admitted with a low chuckle that sent a shiver of nervous excitement up her back, "but I don't live here. I try to get up once or twice a month, it's nice to be able to put the city behind every once in a while. This your first time?"

Lurielle nodded, knowing the heat flushing her cheeks had little to do with the steamy water. "We had a long weekend from work and decided to, um...get away for a few days."

She could see the glint of silver on his tusks as he grinned at her words, settling back against the marble once more. "Well, I'm very pleased that you did. Otherwise, I'd be deprived of such beautiful company on this fine night."

She shifted on the hard marble, feeling her long ears heat. *He's a sweet talker and he probably does this routine with everyone. You're not special.* "I didn't realize you could just have a club membership; we thought everyone lived here full time." He chuckled again and she felt her thighs tremble at the deep, syrupy roll of it. His chest was broad and sculpted, water clinging to the dark hair that dusted his forest-colored skin. His nipples were pebbled in the cooler air above the water, she couldn't help but notice, and Lurielle wondered how he would react if she were to tease the hardened peaks with her tongue.

"There's quite a few who live here full time, but I'm not one of them," he went on with a devilish smile, as though he could divine her thoughts. "That is a *lifestyle* if you know what I mean, and I can't say it's one to which I'm willing to commit full-time." His expressive eyebrows waggled as he spoke, and she was unable to keep her laughter in, blushing again as it echoed around the empty marble hall.

"Do you live very far away then?"

When he mentioned the slightly larger city that bordered Cambric Creek, Lurielle felt her mouth go dry. This man was gorgeous, was funny and charming, and he lived maybe thirty minutes away from her. *He might even be on that dating app of Dynah's...*she realized that he was waiting expectedly for her to answer a question she'd only partially heard. "Oh! Me? Um, we're from Cambric Creek, it's...it's not too far from here."

One of those full eyebrows raised at her stammered answer, the corner of his mouth lifting adorably. "I believe I pass by there on

my way home, one of those little Main Street towns...I'm Kra'khash, by the way. Everyone just calls me Khash. I know that's probably a mouthful for you."

"What's that supposed to mean?" She laughed, fixing him with a look of false indignation, failing to bite back her smile. "Orcish and Elvish aren't *that* different." In truth, they were night and day different, she thought, the guttural Orcish language always sounding harsh to her ears, but she wasn't about to let him know that.

He snorted, leaning back on his elbows, giving her several more inches of his body to ogle. "You all have those delicate, frilly names that sound like poetry and flowers. I'll bet your name is something like Bluebell."

Lurielle hoped that her skin was at least flushing evenly as she shook with laughter. This wasn't anything like what she'd envisioned happening this weekend, but she was enjoying herself immensely. "It's not, you jerk," she wheezed. "My name's Lurielle."

"Lurielle..." His syrupy drawl clung to the L, caressing over the second syllable and leaning on the final L once more, enunciating slowly, as if he were tasting the shape of her name. Lurielle felt her stomach tighten, somehow able to *feel* the drag of his tongue, the curl of those pillowy lips. She bit her own in response, wanting nothing more than to hear her name in his slow drawl again. "Well, that sounds like a song. A pleasure to make your acquaintance, *Lurielle*."

♥♥♥

Ris scanned the deck from her position in the hot tub, not seeing Lurielle anywhere. *She probably left*. From her position in the hot tub, sandwiched between bodies, she scowled in annoyance, wishing she'd stayed with her friend instead of embarking on the doomed mission to get lucky. She'd managed to get the two orcs with whom she'd been flirting out of their clothes and into the hot tub at last...but six other women had immediately joined them: a trio of werecats, an inebriated harpy, and other assorted nymphs and goblins, all angling for the same thing.

This isn't the kind of gangbang I wanted. Too many fucking tourists. She knew that she'd have to make the first move again—if nothing else, these orcs were very conscious of consent, and the plethora of bold tourists meant they could sit back and wait. Ris knew if she climbed into one's lap, she'd likely be jockeying for position with one of the other giggling sightseers before she even got a chance to take a ride. The deck around them still pressed with people: plenty of hangers-on looking to get laid. *Tomorrow you can score an orc. Tonight you just need to get lucky*.

Ris hoped that Lurielle hadn't had a terrible time, that she and Silva were at least comfortable in the room, half wishing she was there with them as she climbed out of the hot tub, noting ruefully that the two orcs barely seemed to notice. The gnoll who'd bought them drinks was still hovering around the pool, and it was he that she approached, gratified to see his eyes widen and mouth open hungrily at the sight of her wet, naked, nearing body. *He's not an orc, but he'll do...for now.*

♥♥♥

"And how did you wind up abandoned by your friends this evening?"

Silva drained the last of her drink, twirling a strand of her long hair around a finger. Tate's eyes moved on a circuit: following the motion of her finger with that sharp-edged smile, meeting her eye, his own seeming to glitter beneath the pub's lights, and scanning the area around the pool tables and the orcs clustered there, before moving back to her. He seemed quite insensible to the growing group of women at the high top tables and at the bar, and Silva preened under his attention.

She hmphed at his words, taking the glass he'd been sipping slowly from. Whatever he'd ordered for her wasn't quite as strong as the Mirúlvin she was used to, and a bowl of peppery, baked wheat crisps had been placed before her, which she steadily munched from, ensuring she wasn't drinking on a half-empty stomach. She'd not had this much to drink in some time, but was pleased to find she'd retained the tolerance built during her short-lived university independence. One of Tate's dark brows arched as she raised the glass to her own lips, his smile twitching.

"I wasn't abandoned. *Someone* told them about the bar at the resort pool, and that's where they were going. I didn't want to spend the night being groped by nudists!"

"You came to the wrong vacation spot, in that case."

"I don't usually come to places like *this* either, you know." She felt a giddy rush as musical laughter bubbled out of him, his dark golden eyes sparkling. Tate perched on the seat beside her, the heel of one of his scuffed, pointed-toe boots hooked on one of the stool's rungs. He was close enough for her to feel the brush of his other outstretched leg and the heat of his breath as he leaned in; close enough to see the long, dark fringe of ebony lashes framing his almond-shaped eyes. There was something Puckish about him, the glint of his teeth and the sparkle in his eyes, a mischievous energy that he seemed to radiate, and Silva felt her pulse race in excitement as he laughed, leaning closer.

"Aye, is that just so? Strange, dove...the evidence of that doesn't *quite* add up."

Tate made a show of straightening the collection of glasses lined up on the polished bartop before her, his smile stretching at her squeal of protest. She had noticed that the big orc tending bar had stayed well away from their corner, only coming to pour them another round when Tate called out to him, doing so with averted eyes before quickly retreating to the other end of the bar once more. The collection of glasses before them had grown as she drained glass after glass of the sweet, golden alcohol, and the relative privacy afforded by the bartender's lack of attentiveness had boosted her courage, even if it did mean the bar before them remained unbussed.

"Some of those are yours!" she protested with a laugh, pushing lightly against one of his wide shoulders. He was slight and angular compared to the crowd of hulking bodies pressed around them, but still broad and muscular compared to the elves she normally dated,

and she was having an increasingly difficult time keeping herself from touching his chest, his arms, his solid thighs.

One of his long, leanly-muscled arms encircled her, resting lightly on the back of her chair, and under normal circumstances, Silva might have felt trapped. Considering where she was and the surrounding company, however, the protective circle of his arm only buoyed her confidence further, secure in the knowledge that none of the massive, lumbering orcs around the pool tables would approach her, with the bonus of providing unfettered access to his smooth, pale green skin.

"Two," he corrected, affording her a glimpse of even more of his sharp-looking teeth, "*two* of these are mine. This," he tapped the side of half-empty glass in front of her, "would have been three, but it seems to have been absconded with."

"You were drinking it very slowly! I thought you were finished!"

He laughed again at her bold-faced lie, like the pealing of a crystal bell, silvery and clear. "So if you don't patronize establishments *like this*–I'll pretend not to be offended, by the way–how, I wonder, did such a bitty little elf learn to drink like a middle-aged troll on midsummer holiday?"

"In my sorority," she admitted with a giggle, gratified at the way his eyes sparkled with amusement. "I was our team anchor for all the drinking games, and we always won."

"Anar Ilse?" he guessed, naming her sorority's biggest rival. He wasn't right, but there was no way an orc would know such specific Elvish conventions...

"You *are* an elf!" Silva exclaimed triumphantly, thrilled that her suspicion was confirmed. He'd side-stepped her earlier question, only saying she "had the right of it," and she'd been too drunk off the wideness of his smile and the light pressure of his hand at her back to press at the time, but now she was unable to hold back. "I *knew* it! Not Anar. I was Ilma Ilma Ullum."

She was about to ask which side of his family bore Elvish blood, marveling that she was actually meeting an elf of mixed-blood in the first place, considering how rare it was to marry outside of one's own community, but Tate interrupted her before the question could form on her lips.

"In that case, I'm certain you absolutely do *not* frequent places like this." One of his slim black brows arched, and his smile once more took on the guise of a smirk. "Ilmarë cotillions and croquet would be more fitting for the pretty princess, I'd wager."

"That's true, mister knows-everything," she admitted, holding his eye defiantly, "and if I'm a princess, you have to answer my questions. You *are* Elvish, aren't you?"

Tate took his time answering. The arm braced around her dropped, and his huge hand closed over her own, slowly stroking the inside of her wrist with the pad of his thumb before meeting her eye with a small sigh.

"Aye. I was raised by my mother's kin. Silmë elves. My father was an orc."

"Oh," she breathed, her voice barely a whisper. "*I'm* a Silmë elf."

It was silly that the knowledge somehow made him even more attractive, but she couldn't help the way her stomach flipped at his words. The featherweight pressure on her wrist continued unabated, and Silva wondered if he could feel the way her pulse jumped from his touch, as she pressed her thighs together.

"An exceptionally beautiful one," he murmured, prying her fingers from the glass she'd taken from him. "My mother," he continued, draining the remains of the glass with a tip of his head, "was half-fae. If I were a betting man, and I am, dove, I'd confidently wager that's a shade more scandal than a lovely little Silmë elf can handle in one evening."

There was something different in his lilting voice, a note of clipped finality that shook her from her giddy stupor, and her forehead creased as he began to gather the array of glasses before her, pushing them to the back edge of the bar for collection.

"If you're going to pretend to know everything, you should try being right," she blurted, wrapping her fingers around his wrist, staying his hand. Silva of the night time, the girl she'd been at school, particularly after she'd loosened up a bit with some liquid courage, was fearless and bold with a carefree laugh, and she was not ready to say goodnight.

He *was* right—it would have been an incredible scandal at the club, to be mixed with not one but *two* different species, even more, to have even an ounce of true fae blood! She remembered reading that elves had once been the favored consorts of the high fae, favor which had been rescinded as the centuries passed and Elvish life-spans grew shorter. A terrible scandal, but she'd not admit that to him, and besides, it didn't matter to her. "You might have grown up with other elves, but you don't know me."

Tate cocked his head, clearly amused by her response. She thought the fae blood in him explained that terrifying smile as it stretched once more, but rather than giving her pause, as it absolutely should have, Silva found herself leaning closer.

"Are you the kind of faerie who collects names?" She crossed her ankles demurely, brushing her toes against his leg as she did so, and gave him her most innocent look. "Do I belong to you now?"

He huffed out another small laugh with a shake of his head, calling out to the bartender. Silva didn't understand the words the two men exchanged in the guttural Orcish language, but the glasses before her vanished, the bar wiped down. She didn't understand the words they spoke, but Silva could tell they were friendly and familiar, a surprise considering the way they'd been avoided. The grizzled orc mumbled as he turned away, quickly retreating back to the other end of the bar, but her companion hadn't missed his words.

"Best be sleepin' with one eye open, boyo," Tate called to his back, and the big orc laughed, a rough scrape of a sound as Tate turned back to her. "Strictly speaking? Yes, I suppose I am...but your name is safe from me, dove. Can't say I find names very interesting."

"Hmm, that's not very exciting of you. What *do* you collect?" The breath she'd been taking stuck in her lungs then, as his hand pressed to the center of her back and his head lowered. Exhilaration rippled through her, culminating in a tingle of arousal between her thighs as

he traced her lips with the tip of his finger before moving his mouth to her ear. He smelled like sandalwood, spicy and warm, but there was something else there as well, something wild and crisp, something that made her want to dart her tongue out like a kitten and taste his skin, which was *completely* untoward, and not the kinds of thoughts an elf of good breeding should be having.

"Secrets," he breathed into her ear, that tingle between her thighs turning into a constant ripple. The loose strands of his silken hair brushed her cheek, his breath was a molten heat on her neck, and when the needle-like pierce of one of his crowded teeth grazed her earlobe, Silva thought she might slide off the barstool in a flood of arousal. "I collect secrets, dove. Shh...that's a secret."

When he released her, sitting up to scan the pool tables again, she gripped the bar tightly, gasping for air that her lungs suddenly felt like they'd been denied. Before her, a tall glass of ice water sat where her collection of empty glasses had been. *Get a grip! You're acting like a human!*

"We're switching to water?" she asked weakly, taking a small sip from the icy-cold glass.

"Aye, we are." His big hand raised, long fingers pushing a lock of hair behind her long, pointed ear. "Because I'd very much like to kiss you, little dove, but I need to know you're not completely off the lash first."

Silva choked out a laugh, taking up the glass and swallowing another gulp. He wasn't what her grandmother would consider a good match, but Silva of the night time didn't need to care. There was something strangely appealing about him, about his shining eyes and that terrifying smile, and she wanted to learn more of his secrets. She was, she decided, taking another gulp of the water, very glad she'd decided to go wandering that night.

♥♥♥

"We're going to chalk today up to being a learning experience," Ris called out, dropping her bag on the floor inside the door. "We've got to beat the other sightseers, or else we need to get these guys on their own somewhere. Otherwise, we're never getting laid."

The gnoll had been satisfactory. He'd been overeager and too excited, hadn't been able to go more than one marginally satisfying round. Still, he'd kept his thick finger circling against her as he'd thrusted into her from behind, the resulting orgasm being good enough. She'd not come all this way for good enough, Ris reminded herself. Tomorrow needed to be better.

"Did you guys just stay in? Luri? Silva?"

As she turned away from the small refrigerator, tipping back half a bottle of water, Ris realized the small apartment was still and silent. "Hello?"

The bedrooms were empty, and the small living room was abandoned. She was the first one back for the night.

"Un-fucking-believable."

♥♥♥

"There are jets!" Lurielle exclaimed with a little shriek, feeling the water burst against her thigh. The echo of her laughter around the marble room no longer made her cringe; she'd been in the steaming pool of water with Khash for close to an hour, laughing for the majority of it.

He worked in finance, she'd learned, was the middle child of a family of seven, had grown up in a small Orcish community in the deep South, where he'd lived until grad school. He played a brutish-sounding popular Orcish sport on weekends that he explained was similar to rugby; he lived in a high-rise apartment building in the city with his bullmastiff but was house hunting for a home of his own. The easy back-and-forth of their conversation possessed none of the awkwardness she'd experienced with guys before, none of the silences and strained laughter she would have expected from a first meeting. It was the nicest date she'd ever been on, Lurielle thought with a massive pang of regret, wishing she'd met him someplace else, someplace that was *meant* to be a date and not an anonymous hook-up. *He's here to relax and get laid, not meet someone.* He'd essentially said so when she'd mentioned the spots the cute server has advised them to check out.

"Too crowded and noisy for my tastes," he'd laughed in that deep, sticky-sweet rumble he had. He visited the hamlet once or twice a month but made little use of the resort amenities, from the sound of it. "There's a beautiful lake, just down that way...much nicer than a pool. We're surrounded by hundreds of acres of countryside. If I wanted to sit on a deck, I could do that from home. There are some excellent restaurants in town, just as good if not better than in the city. And occasionally, I get to enjoy some beautiful company for the evening."

The smile he sent across the bath seemed to melt something inside of her, and Lurielle twisted at his words, knowing that she was being patently idiotic.

"Just occasionally?" She kept her voice and smile light, and her eyes turned to the water, avoiding his hooded gaze. "Handsome brute like you? I find that hard to believe."

His deep chuckle was an echo through a canyon, a rumble of a distant storm, low and vibrating, tugging at her core. "I suppose you and your friends just came for the wine tasting? I happen to know Cambric Creek has some beautiful wineries; I was at one not too long ago on a date. It had the meanest ol' gryphon you've ever looked at twice, but he made a hell of a cab sauv."

His drawling cadence clung to each word, lengthening the vowels into something warm and seductive, despite the way the words themselves made Lurielle's stomach clench once more.

"No, I suppose we didn't," she murmured. "You hear lots of stories about places like this, and it all sounds amazing, but...I don't know. I got out of a long relationship a few years ago and I haven't been out with anyone since, so I guess I don't really know what I was looking for coming here...not a poolside gangbang, though. That's why I was walking back to my room tonight—alone."

When she looked up, Lurielle found Khash's hooded eyes fixed on her, a wistful-looking smile on his full mouth. "Well, that's a song

I know all the words to...and look at that, you happened upon one of my little homemade signs, advertising a pruney orc in an empty bath. My plan worked perfectly."

Her laughter echoed across the marble, and as she shifted on the bench, the burst of water hit her thigh. "Oh! There's another one! There are jets!" The water jets in the thermae were nothing like the roiling bubbles of the hot tubs on the deck that she'd spied with trepidation earlier, were just enough to keep the steamy water circulating and temperate, she realized.

"There are indeed, you just finding one?"

"No one *told* me there were jets," she giggled, flicking water in his direction. "You'd think someone who's all pruney would have introduced the amenities of the tub."

Khash had tipped his head back against the marble, sliding down into the water up to his shoulders, a massive forest-hued shadow beneath the surface. His eyelashes were dark and full against the top of his cheek as he closed his eyes, smiling serenely.

"Yes, ma'am, there are jets. I've been sittin' on one. Hittin' me right in the sweet spot." His eyes popped open at the sound of her outraged laughter and the water flicking over his face, giving her a wolfish smile. "I'm happy to share, you know. Unless you like that big lonely bench there."

There was a faint line through the side of one of his heavy brows—a scar she hadn't noticed from across the tub, thin and trailing down to his temple. As she settled at his side, Lurielle was able to see the slim silver cuffs in his long ears; was able to admire the sharp edge of his sideburns and the loose plait of his hair. The hand that came out of the water was massive, and could easily cup her entire head. Instead, one of his thick fingers traced over her nose, brushing her freckles.

"I couldn't see these from way over there," he murmured, caressing the full apple of her cheek. His honeyed drawl was even sweeter with his warm breath on her face, and Lurielle held her breath, anticipating the moment his full lips met hers. "Pretty as a flower..."

Thick and full and warm, his lips were a gentle press against hers, and she gasped in a breath as they met and parted over and over again. She touched the tip of his tongue with her own tentatively, inviting entrance, and was not disappointed when the hot glide pushed into her mouth. That big hand had dropped to her hip, holding her close to his side as he explored her mouth, tongues dancing.

"How did it go?" she gasped once they'd parted.

The vast expanse of his chest was firm beneath her hands, fingers sliding over those pebbled nipples, the grunt he gave in response sending a tingle through the heat between her thighs.

"I thought that was very nice," he grinned. "I'd like to do it again."

"No," Lurielle clarified, running her palm down his abdomen, feeling his stomach muscles bunch and dance beneath her palm, "your date at the winery. How did it go?"

Her breath hitched when he lifted her to sit on his enormous thigh, her entire mouth fitting easily between his thick tusks as he

kissed her again, his gleaming teeth tugging at her full lower lip when he pulled away again.

"She didn't like dogs. Ordo and I are a package deal, so not very well."

His long, thick fingers massaged circles into her full hip, squeezing the side of her pudgy thigh, and Lurielle took her turn to nip at his pillowy lip, feeling him grip and squeeze a handful of her ample rear.

"I have a Yorkie. She's staying with my neighbor this weekend."

"A little flower and her bunny rabbit," he crooned, smiling against her neck as she laughed in outrage. "I'll bet her name is Lilypiddles." Khash spun her in his arms so that her back was flush against his broad chest, a big hand splayed at her stomach, another cupping her heavy breasts. Lurielle didn't have a chance to feel self-conscious over the softness of her body and her excess flesh, for he was kissing his way down her neck, making her gasp.

"Are we both consenting adults, *Lurielle*?"

His thick drawl slid over her name, a meaty finger sliding beneath her bikini bottom as soon as she breathily agreed. Lurielle let her head drop against his shoulder as Khash wasted no time stroking through her slick folds, circling over that hooded pearl of nerves until she bucked against his hand.

"So wet for me, little flower."

She remembered the sight of his cock, thick and bobbing as he'd emerged from the lake that afternoon, and reached into the water, seeking its turgid length. Her small hand didn't fit around its circumference, but she did her best, pumping the heavy shaft, feeling the smooth glide of his foreskin move over the swollen head. His deep groan of pleasure rumbled against her back, and she tightened her grip in response. The time spent in his company had flown by all too quickly, and this carnal lust-induced interlude was no different, Lurielle thought as she hurtled towards her peak, the two fingers he'd worked into her curling and pressing, making her cry out, her voice echoing through the marbled hall once more. *Hitting the sweet spot...*

"Are you going to come for me, Lurielle?"

He worked her clit with precision, and in a distant corner of her mind, she was reminded that this was a man who absolutely knew what he was doing, was incredibly skilled in the bedroom; who probably *never* went to bed alone...but the rising coil of tension he was building was close to snapping. His big forearm moved like a piston, thick fingers pumping into her as his thumb moved against that sensitive bud, and Lurielle felt herself tipping over the edge, following the promise of his syrupy voice, coating her name the way her slick coated his fingers.

All too soon she was clenching around him, her cry of pleasure embarrassingly loud as she arched off his lap, her thick thighs and fat ass forgotten, her discomfort at the pool bar forgotten, the whole world forgotten as she entered a realm of pure white light, climaxing endlessly against him until everything went black and she ceased to exist.

♥♥♥

"Are you okay to walk, darlin'?"

Lurielle staggered, leaning heavily on the well-muscled arm which supported her, the bright lawn lights of the resort looming ahead. "Wha-where...Khash?"

He grinned down at her, clucking his tongue. She realized she was wrapped in a massive orc-sized towel, her blue pareo over the same well-muscled arm.

"Dainty little Bluebell. You passed out from the heat; we shouldn't have stayed in as long as we did. A crime for which I take full responsibility, even if the conversation was too scintillating to focus on the time. I already got some water in you, but when you get back to your room, I want you to drink a big, cold glass, understand?"

The heat? She'd remembered the heat, the steaming thermae tub, the feeling of his hands on her, and the incredible orgasm she'd had right before she'd—

"I-I didn't finish you! I-but...the heat?"

His warm, rumbling laugh nearly made her knees buckle again.

"Go in. Water, young lady, and a cool room. It's late, and you need some sleep."

Lurielle stared up uncomprehendingly. He was impossibly tall and broad, and she felt dwarfed standing next to him. *He's so handsome...* She squeaked when his big hands landed on her hips, lifting her easily. "I enjoyed spending time with you, Lurielle. I hope to see you again. Good night, darlin'."

♥♥♥

His lips were sweet, she thought, sweet like the golden alcohol that she'd drained, glass after glass. The litany of Elvish curses that fell from his mouth as she licked up the seam of his glans were as equally sweet, his cock jerking against her lips.

She hadn't resisted when he'd kissed her, pushing away the Silva she was—Silva of the daylight hours, chronically preoccupied with perfection, worried about what her grandmother might say and think, worried about finding a good job, worried about having friends and finding a boyfriend who was husband-material.

The tip of one of his long fingers had traced the angle of her jaw, dragging down her throat before tipping her chin up. The noise of the bar suddenly seemed very far away; the crack of balls on the pool table and the big orcs surrounding them, the high-pitched laughter from the table of scantily-dressed goblins near the center of the room and the clink of glasses behind the bar—it had all faded as Tate tilted her face up, his eyes glittering with mischief. Silva had the distinct impression of being underwater, as though they were suddenly invisible to the rest of the world. *Fae magic.* His lips were sweet and his teeth were sharp when they nipped lightly at her lower lip, before it was sucked between his own. She couldn't explain the electricity that seemed to crackle through her veins as the kiss deepened; once, twice, the slide of his tongue against hers overwhelming her on the third. She'd thought him handsome hours earlier when she'd been an uptight mouse, but then she was free to *be*, and kissed him without hesitation.

The wild, sandalwood smell of him had made her dizzy when

he'd leaned over her afterward, guiding her hands as she'd lined up a shot on the pool table. She'd giggled as the cue ball gave a satisfying crack against a cluster of stripes, feeling his sharp teeth graze her neck lightly and his erection press into her back.

"Is it hard to juggle?" she'd asked, shivering at the light touch of his fingertips, ghosting against her skin at the back of her neck. "Does your family have different expectations for how they expect you to be?" Silva was all too fluent in familial expectations, after all, and sympathized immensely.

"It can be, I suppose..."

Tate's smile had widened once more, that fae glint of too many teeth, giving her the impression of a great maw that could open wide and swallow her up. "For example, little dove, right now the Orcish part of me wants to see those beautiful lips of yours wrapped around my cock, while the Fae in me wants to keep you on your knees until I'm through with you, but the Elvish part is too much of a gentleman to ever say such crass things to a lass as lovely as yourself."

The bar's backroom had another pool table and was lined with several low sofas, battered but surprisingly clean, and blessedly empty. Silva felt lighter than air as she followed him through the doorway, giggling as she landed gracelessly atop him on the worn upholstery. His breath stuttered when she bit at his neck, her fingers nimble and sure as she undid the buckle of his belt, faltering only as he sucked at the jumping pulse at her throat, hard enough to leave a bruise. *A lady always packs a scarf for such occasions...*

His honeyed eyes were lit with delight when she slid to the floor and licked a broad stripe up his shaft, the light green darkening gradually towards the tip, and his musical laughter broke off on a hiss when she revealed the swollen glans, suckling at the seam she exposed there. Deep green, edged in pink, he was sweet there as well, his sharp burst of laughter ending in a groan as she swallowed his cock, tightening her lips as her head bobbed.

She'd been good at *this* once as well, she remembered, moving her tongue over the pulsing vein she'd discovered as she sucked, feeling his fingers grip her hair and his hips raise to meet her mouth. Her jaw was just beginning to ache when he pulled her back, his smile still wide.

"Keep that up and it'll not be my fault when I fill your mouth, dove."

Silva pulled herself from the floor and straddled his waist in one fluid movement, meeting his lips roughly. He had lovely green skin and glossy black hair, but there was more than just a hint of the fae about him, she thought as he gripped her hips, reaching beneath her skirt and pushing her delicate, lace-edged panties aside, fingers sliding through her slickened folds. *More fae than orc by far.*

She wondered if it was fae magic, the way he seemed to know *just* the right angle in which to press the two long fingers he'd slid into her, rubbing against a spot within her she'd never been able to reach on her own and had only discovered on accident: a breathy, blissful experience with a previous boyfriend that he'd unwittingly managed exactly once, never to replicate the sensation again. Tate, by contrast,

seemed to find the spot with ease. A repetitive stroking within, as his thumb circled that sensitive bud of nerves at the top of her sex; a tandem rhythm that left her gasping, the tension behind her navel tightening like a band, growing more taught with every pass of his long digits until it snapped. Silva arched as she climaxed, her head dropping back, feeling the room spin.

He sucked his fingers clean once she'd clenched around them, her face pressed to the side of his long neck, gasping her pleasure at the way he'd played her body like a musical instrument; Silva of the daytime, of worries and expectations, gone, for the moment.

The smell of his skin was intoxicating, and she breathed in deeply, not wanting to leave the seclusion of this room. She rolled the condom he produced onto him herself before sinking down on his throbbing length, rolling her hips against him in an increasing frenzy until she cried out once more, before he flipped her to her back.

She wondered if Ris and Lurielle had found what they were looking for that night, tightening her legs around Tate's hips as he fucked her, here in this comfortable little room in the bar where everyone kept their clothes on. It was a shame, she thought, as he came with a shudder, that she'd not gotten to taste him, wondering if his release would have been as sweet as his lips.

Perhaps she would come back tomorrow, as her friends once more sought adventures with the nudists, to let him fill her mouth after all.

♥♥♥

how's it going so far?

is the place crawling with hotties?

I'm so mad at myself for not going!

promise me we can go back, ok??

Ris huffed in annoyance at the text message. Dynah—despite her frequent inability to follow through on things, like this weekend—was a vibrant chatterbox, flirtatious and funny and fearless, and would have been good company on this trip. Ris loved Lurielle dearly, and Silva was sweet and sunny, but prim and proper seemed too modest a descriptor for their younger co-worker, and when it came to actually engaging with any of the burly nudists, Lurielle's feet seemed to have caught a chill.

Alas, Dynah, like Silva, was feeling the daily pressure to get married and give her mother a grandchild. *Unlike* Silva, Dynah was casting the widest net she possibly could. She'd persuaded Ris to join an interspecies dating app with her, touting it as an exciting way to meet guys without needing to go trolling the bar scene. Three months and nothing but a handful of marginally satisfying hookups later, Ris was convinced Dynah had trapped her in the age-old tradition of misery loving company.

Trapping herself in a relationship with a guy like the intolerably entitled dragon-born, for whom Dynah had missed the trip, seemed like settling for a slow, painful death; a punishment with which she was not willing to sentence herself. That didn't mean she wasn't open to

meeting someone. Dating was a numbers game, that's what she'd always been told. If she waded through enough conceited elves and lecherous werewolves, she'd find someone who appreciated her; someone smart and sexy who was okay with a lack of serious commitment...the slog in the meantime, however, was becoming tedious.

The doorknob rattled and she froze. On the other side of the door, she heard a keycard beep and fail, beep and fail, before Lurielle came staggering through the door on the third attempt, wrapped in an oversized beach towel. "Water," she croaked, making her way unsteadily towards the kitchen.

"What happened to you?!" Ris hurried to the small kitchen, pulling two overpriced bottles of water from the fridge. The fruity drinks served at the poolside bar were egregiously strong and gaggingly sweet, a far cry from the perfectly mixed cocktails they'd enjoyed at dinner, and it hadn't taken long to realize just why the harpy was staggering around the dancefloor. As Lurielle unscrewed the bottle with unsteady hands, Ris made a mental note that tomorrow night's activities ought to be undertaken sans libations. "I thought you'd headed back to the room! Are-are you okay? Do you think you need to throw up?"

Lurielle shook her head vigorously, reaching out to steady herself on the counter before gulping down a quarter of the bottle. "No, I-I'm not drunk. There are steam tubs, Roman baths, and I...I stayed in too long. I'm just dehydrated, I'm fine. Can breakfast please not be at the crack of dawn tomorrow?"

Ris huffed, unsurprised by the request. She was used to being the only morning person on trips, and Lurielle came hustling into work with only minutes to spare at least once a week. "Fine, but then I want to hear everything! Did you see Silva in the lobby? I can't believe she's not already tucked into bed."

"She's probably down there...where else would she have gone?"

It seemed unlike Silva to not be in the room, she thought as Lurille's door closed with a click. *You ought to go find her. She's probably downstairs, just let her know everyone's back.* She wondered, as she crossed the room to the windows if Silva was going to spend the entire weekend sitting in the resort lobby.

Pushing back the sheers, her attention was immediately caught by a dark shape in the lawn. Bathed in moonlight, the long shadow grew in length as the lumbering figure drew closer. Ris could see it was an approaching orc and that he'd be crossing the lawn directly in front of their balcony. *And you'll be there to meet him.* The magenta cover-up would do, she decided, nearly vaulting over the small sofa to reach her room. *You can go looking for Silva after you talk to him*. She was down the balcony steps and across the lawn like a shot, just in time for the huge orc to come lumbering into view at the top of one of the crests in the hilly lawn. Ris flashed her most dazzling smile, knowing the open-weave poncho left absolutely nothing to the imagination. Silva was probably sitting in the well-lit lobby reading a book, she told herself as the orc before her slowed. *Time to recoup this night...*

♥♥♥

Her room was bathed in moonlight as she turned to the bed, dropping the bundled pareo to the floor. She ought to take a hot shower, wash out the frizzy mess the thermae had left of her hair, and rinse out her swimsuit, but all she was able to manage was struggling out of the wet bottoms, cursing when it rolled around her thick thighs, eventually freeing herself and kicking them off. The wet top joined the bottoms on the floor, and Lurielle climbed beneath the cool hotel sheets, still clinging to his oversized towel.

His lips had been soft and warm as they pressed to hers, the chocolate pits of his hooded eyes almost seeming liquid in the resort's bright lights. She wasn't sure how she made it up to her room, wasn't entirely sure what she'd said to Ris as she staggered into the apartment, mumbling about overheating at the empty thermae and passing out. She drank a bottle of water, as he'd instructed, and took another to her room where she dropped into bed.

It had been too long since she'd been with someone and she was too out of practice, her heart too easily caught. If she would have joined that stupid dating app with Ris and Dynah, maybe she'd be past this point, able to meet men and go about her business without a care...but she hadn't, and she wasn't. The reclamation of her life hadn't included finding someone to love, not yet. Not until she lost more weight, became more interesting, more confident... *I'm working on myself right now* had been her excuse for far too long.

She was supposed to be having a fun weekend with her friends; she was supposed to be enjoying the sight of naked men and having cheap, meaningless sex. *You weren't supposed to meet someone real.*

Lurielle pulled the sheet up to her chin, closing her eyes stubbornly, willing sleep to claim her to keep the tears that burned her eyes at bay. She rolled to her side, pressing her face to the pillow, a syrupy-thick, drawling voice playing at her ear, unaware of the crumpled slip of paper within the tangle of her blue pareo on the floor.

PLAYORC
FOR YOUR PLEASURE !!
ORC SIZED!
02

Part 02

♥ *The Big Night* ♥

The sky above the hills was a perfect, unblemished blue, without a cloud in sight. The only sound was birdsong, only occasionally broken by the hum of an engine coming from the parking lot.

She wondered, as she stretched into a cobra pose, if the nudists ever vacated the premises, leaving the resort to be just a pretty hotel tucked in the scenic landscape. It would be a nice weekend away, to do yoga in the sunshine and make a dent in her to-be-read pile. Ris closed her eyes, breathing into the pose, imagining herself on her mat in one of the open fields, instead of the small balcony.

She'd started yoga after going to a drop-in beginner class with Dynah several years earlier.

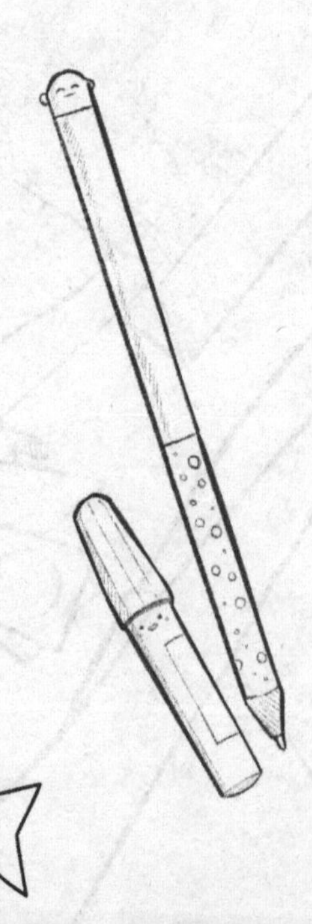

Dynah, in typical Dynah fashion, had lost interest once the handsome yogi had been replaced by a female counterpart, but Ris had stayed on, finding the practice beneficial to her running and more enjoyable than Elvish liltenu. She'd attended a liltenu class as well, shortly after her move to Cambric Creek, thinking she ought to make a place for herself in the Elvish community. The aerobic stretching class had been filled with the sort of elves she'd grown up with, both Summerland and Silmë: coolly reserved and identically pretty, in uniforms of expensive leggings and glossy, high-end hair extensions. They'd whispered together with bent heads for the duration of the class, and she'd quickly determined that carving a place in their ranks would be easier said than done.

It wasn't that she didn't have the practice. She'd grown up going to Elvish schools, with Elvish friends, and none of her friends across the many years would have been able to guess she was from a different social stratum as them. Private school had taught her to be friendly and confident and covert in her maneuvering. When the girls at school would come back from summer recess with stories of exotic travels and expensive-sounding lessons, Ris would glibly describe her family's time away at their *summer home*, and all it entailed: the equestrian dancing lessons she was forced to endure and the endless lobster dinners prepared by the help, stories that were light on specifics and heavy on ornamentation, before deftly turning the conversation back to boys in their class, which was what everyone wanted to talk about anyways.

None of them needed to know her family spent two weeks every summer in a cozy rented cottage in a tiny coastal town, or that her *equestrian lessons* came by the way of a toothless old centaur who wrangled equally toothless old ponies, taking the handful of budget tourists to ride on the slowly plodding horse's backs through the ankle-deep surf; nor that the banquet dinners she was forced to attend were actually lobster rolls wrapped in foil and dripping in butter, takeaway purchased from a grizzled crabmer's stand on the pier. Her shoes and purses were purchased from second-hand consignment shops far from home, afternoons spent scouring racks with her mother, and because she was popular, her unique style was coveted: elves on the edges of her social circle begging their grandmothers for their own trendy, vintage shoulder bags. University was easier, to a degree, but she always found a way to fit in, to blur the edges of who she was and who they thought she was until pretty, popular Ris was all that remained.

The Elvish community in Cambric Creek was particularly insular, old families and older money, and she realized, after attending a welcome event at the Elvish social club, that she no longer had the desire to twist herself into something she wasn't. The town community center offered a full slate of classes and clubs; she joined the multi-species gym and had no regrets.

This resort would be perfect for a retreat...if only they had a spa.

The suite was silent when she tiptoed through it, with no sound coming from either Lurielle or Silva's rooms. By the time she'd come

back from her brief dalliance with the orc outside their balcony, the light had been on under Silva's door, clicking off shortly thereafter. *She probably nodded off by the fireplace*, Ris thought as she passed through the lobby a few minutes later. The morning was cool, and the wide lawn in front of the resort glittered with dewdrops in the early-morning light. It would be a hot afternoon, but it was perfect weather for a run.

The town was similarly quiet and empty: the shops and restaurants dark, all of the tourists and orcs still sleeping off the previous night's activities. It wasn't until she'd turned up one of the small, shop-lined streets, passing an apiarist and a soap maker's boutique, that she saw another sign of life in the form of a tall, leggy orc. She was half a block away, but Ris could clearly hear his words, as he bellowed dramatically in the middle of the sidewalk.

"You would disband the hallowed bonds of fellowship between us? 'He that is thy friend indeed, He will help thee in thy need.' Words which shall yield a bitter fruit for you to choke on, sir!"

She snorted at his monologue, which she realized was being shouted at someone above as laughter cascaded down the side of the black-bricked building.

"Get your bleedin' car out of my spot, or I'm having it towed," she heard a heavy brogue call down in response. *There must be apartments over the businesses.* "One...two..."

The tall orc didn't wait for three, taking off in a sprint, his own laughter echoing between the deserted buildings.

When she rounded the same corner, she saw him again. Unlike the orcs she knew from home and the ones she met last night, with their long hair and symbolic braids, the sides of this orc's head were shaved, leaving his jet-black hair to flop over to one side, not quite brushing his broad shoulder.

She admired the width of his back, tapering to a narrow waist and ending in those endlessly long legs. She was tall for an elf, and always tended to gravitate to guys who could make her feel dainty. She would come up to the middle of this tall drink of water's chest, a perfect kissing height if she were interested in kissing any of the orcs she met. *It's not that kind of trip...this is to cross stuff off the bucket list, nothing more.*

He'd slowed to a walk at that point, glancing over his shoulder when he heard her approach. She watched him turn back, only to do a double-take, whipping around with a bright smile, stepping to the side of the pavement, allowing her to pass. He wasn't as bulky as the orcs at the poolside party the night before, but his face, from the quick glance she got as she jogged past beaming, was angular and handsome.

"The wine of friendship is succor and light, an oath which brightens the darkest of night."

She tossed the beginning of the Elvish sonnet over her shoulder, grinning when the handsome orc's laughter rang out behind her.

"Beauty *and* brains?! Be still my heart!"

Ris slowed as she approached the corner, giving him an opportunity to catch up, but when she turned, he was gone. She was standing before the little bistro, she realized, where they'd eaten the previous evening. The handsome orc must have turned up the narrow alley she'd passed, on the edge of the restaurant's light-strung terrace. *Maybe he'll be at the party tonight.* There was curling script in the lower corner of the window she stood before, shimmering gold, advertising the champagne brunch she remembered seeing on the menu the previous evening, and she turned back in the direction of the resort to ready herself for the day. *Perfect. They don't want to get up early anyway.*

♥♥♥

"So you just passed out?! That's crazy! Good thing that guy was there, huh?"

Lurielle tightened her grip on the delicate stem of the champagne flute, tipping it back before answering. She didn't know why she was lying. She'd slept in far too late, had woken with a headache, as she always did when she cried before bed, and now she was sitting across from Ris and Silva at brunch, lying about Khash as her head spun from the copious amount of champagne they'd consumed.

"The place last night does a champagne brunch; I saw it on their window," Ris had announced once everyone had emerged from their rooms that morning. "Doesn't that sound scrumptious? Every day should start with champagne!"

She had grunted her approval from where she sprawled on the sofa, feeling like a worn-out sock. Ris looked like a fitness model, by contrast, in her spandex leggings and strappy sports bra, her sleek, straight hair swinging from a high ponytail. Silva had straightened up as Ris spoke, her eyes widening as she nodded her agreement, disappearing back into her room, leaving Lurielle alone to contemplate the frizzy mess atop her head.

Her dreams had been sluggish and thick; a tide of dark, sweet syrup enveloping her and pulling her down as she tossed and turned. She'd woken several times throughout the night, gasping and tangled in her sweat-soaked sheets, the thick curl of his drawling voice still playing at her ear.

When she'd staggered to the kitchen at one point to refill her water glass, wrapped in the big towel she'd come home in, the balcony doors had been open. As she peered out, Lurielle had been able to see Ris, down in the lawn a short distance away, talking to a hulking green shape. Turning back to the kitchen, she'd unexpectedly locked eyes with Silva, slipping through the door soundlessly. Her practically perfect co-worker had looked as neat and put-together as she always did, and Lurielle didn't have the presence of mind to question where she'd been coming from before stumbling back to bed, gripping the side of the borrowed towel tightly. She'd still been clinging to his towel that morning, holding it like a security blanket as bright sunlight filtered in through the window.

"Yeah, good thing," she mumbled, pushing grilled peaches around her plate, her lie evidently accepted. She eyed herself in the mirrored mercury glass column across from their table, wondering if Silva's high-end hair products had diminished the snarled bird's nest effect her hair had assumed as she tossed and turned the night before. Silva had enthusiastically responded to her request for smoothing cream, bringing a salon's worth of product into Lurielle's room, giving her a step-by-step tutorial on the steps in which she ought to use them, before disappearing back to her own room to change her clothes for the third time.

The same jocular server from the previous evening had greeted them when they'd stepped through the door, watching with a sharp-edged smile as a heavily pierced tiefling seated them, quickly filling the blue cut-glass water goblets. When the tiefling girl left to put their order in, Ris had dropped back against the carved wooden chair back with a sigh.

"I'm not going to call last night a bust, but it definitely wasn't a win. We need to do better today, ladies."

Lurielle had kept her gaze trained to the table. The table linens were beautiful, appearing to be hand-embroidered and crisply pressed, a lovely contrast with the eclectic mix of tableware. The entire restaurant was done in soft colors with delicate detailing, flowers and branches and lace, giving the impression of some secret nook in an enchanted forest. She'd noticed Silva also kept her eyes lowered, seemingly engrossed with the pretty water goblet's stems.

"What do you think we should do today?"

"I think," Lurielle started carefully before Ris could suggest going hiking in their lingerie, "that we should hit the shops. There's a really pretty necklace I want to look at in the place that does the hand-forged silver, and the soap shop was right next door. And Silva wanted to find some cider."

Silva's eyes had raised in surprise, a pleased smile on her face. Her little yellow scarf was expertly knotted around her neck in place of her pearls, a perfectly frayed denim jacket atop her periwinkle dress. It was the third outfit she'd changed into that morning after Ris had suggested brunch, and Lurielle wondered if her younger co-worker experienced such manic indecision over her clothes every time she

left the house. She didn't understand how Silva managed to look as polished and perfect as she ever did, despite having come back to the room in the middle of the night, and had been about to ask what she had gotten up to in her and Ris's absence, but the question had been interrupted by the handsome, cocky-looking orc. The stainless steel ice bucket had seemed to smoke on the table as he placed it, and the girls fell silent in anticipation.

"So very nice to see you lovely ladies back again."

His lightly accented voice had the same musical, sing-songy cadence that it had the night before, but something about his smile made Lurielle shiver as he turned away to expertly pop the cork on their champagne. He was short compared to Khash, slim and graceful, but there were *entirely* too many teeth crowding his smile, and their glint seemed sinister in the bright light of day. When he slid the magnum into the bucket of ice after pouring their glasses, his smile twitching at the corner as if he were trying and failing to keep it in check, Ris's eyebrows shot up. "Enjoy, ladies," he'd trilled lightly, before turning away from their table to return to the bar, whistling a jaunty tune.

"Is it supposed to be that big?" Ris had hissed after he'd moved away, gesturing to the bottle. "The menu definitely said 'a bottle of the house champagne,' right? How are we supposed to drink a whole magnum?!" The tiefling had appeared at that moment, bearing their orders, the jewelry in her arched brows coming together in confusion as she eyed the oversized bottle of champagne. "Well, bottoms up, I guess. We can't let it go to waste...good thing we can hold our liquor, right?"

Silva let out a high-pitched peal of laughter at Ris's words, their glasses clinking together musically, and Lurielle watched as the slender orc's head snapped up at the sound from across the room. His sharp smile gleamed like knives and she shivered again, tipping back her glass until the raspberry at the bottom reached her lips, thinking that there was definitely something unnerving about him.

Now though, the bottle was nearly empty, their conversation punctuated by too much laughter, and Lurielle sent a silent thank you across the room to the creepy orc for inadvertently messing up their order and making her whereabouts the previous evening a forgotten afterthought.

"I met a guy last night out on the lawn, after I came back from the pool," Ris slurred, leaning into the table. "He invited us to come to a party tonight, I guess they do a big bonfire down by the cabins. I figured we could eat dinner together before we decide what we want to do?"

"What was his name?" Lurielle blurted, cramming the last peach in her mouth, something to soak up the alcohol sloshing within her. The image of Khash meandering around the resort grounds after he left her, accosting her friend in the moonlight was not one she wished to contemplate, but now that the seed had been planted, her alcohol-soaked mind could envision it perfectly. "Does he live here?"

"He was naked, so I'm assuming he lives here!" Ris laughed, her face screwing up in thought. "You know, now that you mention it, I

don't think I got his name. I was on my knees and it never came up... other things did though!"

She dissolved into giggles, and Lurielle felt her long ears heat, the champagne providing her with the stomach-churning image of Khash's square jaw dropped, his mouth hanging open in pleasure as Ris finished the job Lurielle had started in the thermae, his experience with her forgotten. The tiefling appeared at the table then, depositing a basket filled with fragrant, bready pastries, warm and sweet-smelling. "Did-did we order this?"

"Oh it's-it's a part of the brunch special," the tiefling explained, pulling back the cloth covering to reveal the assortment of croissants and danishes. "And I'm sure you need something to balance that champagne, am I right?" The girl gave them a bright smile as she cleared away their empty plates, "Would anyone care for coffee or tea? I'll get those water glasses refilled..."

Silva gave another squeak of laughter, and Lurielle watched the orc's head rise again from where he worked behind the bar. The tiefling moved from their table, beelining directly to where he stood,, their heads coming together conspiratorially.

"This place is wild," Ris announced, picking out a fat croissant, chocolate oozing from the end. "They gave us a magnum and that brunch menu doesn't say a single thing about pastries...anyway, does it matter about his name? We're just meat to these guys, and that's all they should be to us."

Lurielle sipped from the refilled water goblet, feeling a stone turn over in her stomach, a heavy island in a sea of champagne. *Just a piece of meat*. Ris was right. He was too charming, too funny, far too handsome for her to believe she'd been anything other than just another *sightseer* to him. Best to put him out of mind and try to salvage the rest of the weekend.

Shopping proved to be an uncoordinated adventure, as they staggered down the sidewalk, gripping each others arms and giggling, and they wound up headed back to their room not long after, laden with bags of small trinkets.

"Let's just put our swimsuits on and lie out by the pool," Silva tittered once they arrived back in the suite. "We need to metabolize these mimosas before we try to do anything else."

Lurielle realized her blue two-piece had been left on the floor of her room the night before, leaving her to wear the yellow halter-style she'd packed. Picking up the still-damp scraps of fabric, she brought them to the bathroom to rinse in the tub, turning her friend's words over and over in her mind. *Just a piece of meat.* Ris was right, and she needed to shake off the previous evening. She was here to have a good time, after all. None of these men cared about her, and she didn't need to care about them in return.

The blue pareo was similarly still in a crumpled heap on the floor, where she'd dropped it last night before crawling into bed. The small scrap of paper fluttered from the gauzy folds, disappearing beneath the bed as she grunted in annoyance, dropping to her knees.

His handwriting was strong and bold, with firm downward strokes and long lines, the letters of his name filling the white square, the numbers below it equally as long. She sat on the floor beside the bed, her lungs unable to draw breath, moving her finger over his name until Silva called out that they were ready to head to the pool, snapping her from her reverie. Saving the number in her phone, she placed the small scrap of paper, an indelible piece of him, into her bag, determined not to lose it. She would decide what to do once they were installed in the sun.

Emerging from her room, she saw Silva slipping a sheer-white cover-up over her head, the gossamer fabric doing nothing to disguise her model-perfect body in its pink two-piece. Ris hadn't bothered with an additional layer at all, and her black string bikini left scant little to the imagination, a towel slung over her arm and sunglasses propped on her head. *Are you sure you don't want to put on something a bit more modest, dear? You're going to look so terribly out of place, after all...*she gritted her teeth, forcing her mother's voice out of her head, unwilling to allow the negative thoughts to dampen the elation she felt over the number in her phone.

"Don't forget water, ladies, hydration is important! We want to make sure we have our energy for tonight!" Ris said cheerfully, lowering the sunglasses and throwing open the door. "Let's go!"

♥♥♥

The champagne had been sweet and effervescent, much finer than the acrid, dry stuff that usually constituted as house champagne, the bubbles still making her head feel light, giving her courage she might have lacked otherwise.

Hi. It's Lurielle

Tipping her head back, she let the sun warm her, and attempted

to tune out the shrieks and laughter around them. The pool wasn't as crowded as it had been the night before, although the majority of the sun chairs were full. There were a good amount of other tourists in the pool, and more than a handful of orcs, but it seemed the spectacle of public sex was one reserved for the evening. She knew Ris was right, that she was probably just setting herself up for disappointment...but he didn't *seem* like the kind of guy who treated women like meat. The phone buzzed against her leg and her heart climbed to her throat, waiting.

Saving immediately

"Bluebell"

She breathed around her heart, feeling lightheaded. *It's just the champagne, that's all*...but when her phone buzzed again, she was unable to hold back her smile.

I'm glad you messaged

I was worried I'd frightened you off

Lurielle was certain Silva was going to be able to hear the thump of her heartbeat next from the next chair. She had joked that they'd lined up by height on the sun chairs—tall, leggy Ris, perfectly proportioned Silva, and her—short and stumpy, on the end. There was no reason for her to think someone like him would be interested in someone like her.

I'd like to see you again

Dinner tonight?

The girls had decided to have dinner together before finalizing their plans for the night. Silva had no intention of going to the bonfire, and Ris would not be missing it...she needed to decide which direction she'd be heading in. Closing her eyes behind her sunglasses, Lurielle sucked in a slow breath. She was lying to herself even pretending she didn't want to see him again, that her thoughts hadn't been about him since he'd left her with a soft kiss the previous evening.

I'm having dinner with my friends

But maybe after?

There. No more lying to herself. She didn't want to go with Ris, to be another piece of meat in a loud, overbearing crowd of people; nor was she terribly interested in whatever solitary pursuits Silva was planning.

Drinks and dessert then? I know just the place

Looking forward to it, Bluebell

The address he sent her was on the same street where they'd be having dinner, and she'd meet him once the girls split up. *Now all you have to do is work yourself into a hysteria for the next eight hours over what to wear*, she thought, settling back on her sun chair. The dimple on his chin was adorable. She wondered if his earlobes were sensitive, wondered how different he would look fully dressed. It made her flush to think she hadn't yet seen him with clothes on, such a backward situation. *Stop getting your hopes up, dummy!* Lurielle tried to control her breathing, knowing her internal voice was right. The bloom of warmth in her chest was absolutely from the champagne, had nothing to do with Khash, nothing to do

with her excitement over seeing him again, hearing his slow drawl, feeling the weight of his deep chocolate eyes moving over her.

Nothing at all to do with Khash. It was just the champagne, she told herself, unable to keep the small smile from her face.

♥♥♥

She recognized his impossibly broad shoulders almost immediately.

Khash was sitting at the bar, scrutinizing the menu, giving her a chance to look him over before he noticed her. A dark blue blazer stretched across his wide back, the structural integrity of the sleeves were threatened by his well-defined arms. The bright white of his shirt collar made his deep green skin glow; his thick, black hair plaited into an intricate braid that started at his crown, the kind she'd never once successfully managed to do to her own hair.

He was gorgeous.

Lurielle held her breath for a moment, steeling her nerves before moving around the reception podium to approach him from behind. *You can do this.* "You look like you're reading something in a foreign language," she murmured into his ear. "If it's in Elvish, I can help. I know it's probably a mouthful for you."

She had given herself a stern talking-to on the short walk from the restaurant where the girls had gone their separate ways. *You're not going to get your hopes up. You're not going to act like a smitten idiot. He probably does this with a new girl every time he's here. You're not going to get your hopes up.* Words she'd repeated over and over as she moved up the cobbled sidewalk, but as Khash turned his hooded, chocolate-brown eyes crinkled with his smile she knew she was lost.

"Well now, if it was in Elvish, Bluebell, I'd imagine the whole menu would just be pictures of flowers and fancy lil' cupcakes."

She didn't know how he managed to make *cupcakes* sound like something obscene, but the syrupy pull of his voice tugged

and lengthened every vowel into something seductive and warm, bringing heat to her cheeks as she leaned into him, as far as she could in her dress.

The structured dress was the nicest thing she'd packed: princess-seamed in a heavy, stiff cotton that kept her stomach sucked in and forced her to stand up straighter, with a full skirt that concealed her more-than-generous curves. The wide-set straps highlighted the teensy hint of clavicle she actually possessed, and the sweetheart neckline made her heavy breasts somehow look as perky as she wished they'd been when she was seventeen. The whole thing was an optical illusion, but, Lurielle reasoned, he'd already eyed her in a two-piece and still wanted to see her again. She was glad she'd packed it, as he turned on the stool, obliging her to take a step back as he took her in.

"You look exceptionally beautiful tonight, Lurielle," he purred, his thick drawl making her name sound like something decadent.

Her breath caught as she was reminded again of how tall he was, how wide and muscular, and how small she felt in comparison. It was nice, she decided, having spent too many years feeling like a lumbering lummox next to all of the slender, svelte elves she knew, which was all of them. Khash made her feel dainty, which was *not* a familiar feeling, but still one she liked. His collar was open, the first few buttons of his pristine white shirt unfastened, giving her a view of his thick neck and wide throat, obliging her to restrain herself from pulling him down to her level so that she could feel his pulse jump beneath her lips. A pale blue pocket square was his only accoutrement, besides the gleaming watch face at his wrist, and she touched it lightly, using the excuse of smoothing the lapels of his jacket to run her palms down his broad chest.

"You look very nice in clothes, that's a relief. A bit of a dandy, I see."

His laugh was a slow cascade of amber honey as he took her hand, and Lurielle felt her smile beam as he brushed his lips to her knuckles before leading her to the waiting hostess.

"My granddaddy didn't break his back in the mines for years for me to *not* be a sharp-dressed gentleman. I hope you appreciate how much I'm willing to sacrifice my pantsless time to see you, Bluebell. We can order steak for dessert, right?"

♥♥♥

He was deep in concentration, looking over the bar with his back to the windows. Silva huffed on the sidewalk in frustration, shifting from foot to foot. She'd been standing there in the shadows for close to ten minutes waiting for him to turn and raise his head, but Tate was thoroughly engrossed in his task, the tablet he clutched illuminating his chin as he moved from bottle to bottle.

The restaurant they'd chosen that evening had been across the intersection from the bistro, and she had caught sight of his wide, sharp smile through the small eatery's large windows as soon as their hostess had led them to a table on the flagstone terrace, making

certain to take the chair facing the street. Every time she caught sight of him moving around the bistro's mercury glass-backed bar, Silva felt her heart flutter in anticipation.

At one point, sometime after the stuffed figs she'd ordered for dinner had arrived, she watched him lean over the bar, chatting up the cluster of female patrons sitting before him. Even from across the street, Silva could clearly see his slightly too-wide smile, could almost hear his musical laughter and lilting voice. She wondered if they were elves, before deciding that it didn't matter; wondered if they were pretty, if he was telling them at that moment that he'd be at the little pub on the corner after his shift.

"Silva? Something wrong with the figs?"

Ris's voice snapped her from her thoughts, and she'd realized her fork was hanging in the air, mid-way between the plate and her mouth.

She'd tried to pay attention to the conversation with her friends, to ignore the sight of the handsome half-orc across the street, but it had been hard. She'd never been the jealous type before, and certainly didn't have any standing to act in such a way, but she found the small flame of possessiveness which had flared to life within difficult to extinguish.

She hadn't expected to feel the way she had when he left her the previous night. She supposed it had been the way he'd kissed her, once their dalliance in the bar's backroom was complete. Despite being no stranger to flings and ill-advised one-night stands, Silva couldn't remember any of those partners ever having kissed her as gently as Tate had, cradling her face and smoothing the pads of his thumbs over her temples, tracing her long ears and angle of her jaw. She'd been breathless when he pulled her to her feet at last, his fingers lacing with her smaller ones when they left the little room. Abruptly, the sound of the other bar patrons had come bleeding back, loud and raucous, the underwater sensation vanished.

She'd demurred that he didn't need to walk her back to the resort, but clung to his arm when he insisted, relishing the opportunity to press herself to his side. "I've never liked the dark," she admitted sheepishly after hesitating when he led her up a pitch-black footpath, the moon providing scant illumination through the thick trees.

"Don't worry, dove. There's nothing in the dark that's scarier than me. You'll not be molested on my watch."

The resort had been brightly lit, uplighting illuminating the white-painted frontage and clusters of spotlights in the lawn, creating a bright halo effect around the building. Silva had slowed as they approached, and Tate stopped before the bright lights began, leaving them in shadow.

"I don't know what our plans are for tomorrow, but we don't leave until Sunday," she'd blurted when they arrived at the edge of the wide, circular drive. "Maybe...maybe I'll be free?"

"Maybe so," he'd mused, neither a confirmation nor a refusal. "You know where to find me." He'd raised their still-entwined fingers, kissing the inside of her wrist before releasing her hand to cup her face. His hands were huge; the long, slender fingers spanning her

skull, thumbs gently tracing the contours of her cheeks once more. "Perhaps our paths will cross again, sweet Silva." She'd fairly floated to bed, still able to feel the heat of his mouth as she curled beneath the sheets.

Now she shifted in indecision, wondering if she ought to go back to the room and just forget about this silly infatuation. Silva didn't know how to explain why she felt electricity crackle through her veins when he'd kissed her, nor why she found his mischievous eyes and somewhat terrifying smile so attractive. She was half-convinced that she hadn't yet seen the full extent of those gleaming sharp teeth and wanted to see his smile stretch fully; wanted to feel them graze her neck and mark her skin, wanted him to swallow her down, wanted to learn more of his secrets. *Madness!*

She didn't need the gift of second sight to know her grandmother would be horrified, could picture her pursed lips and disapproving head shake, but Silva of the nighttime didn't need to care, and the indifference was intoxicating. *You should go to the bar. He'll be there eventually, and he'll be happy to see you.* The voice in her head seemed to direct her feet, and before she quite realized what she was doing, the creaking black door to The Plundered Pixie was before her.

There was an orc outside the entrance with endlessly long legs, leaning on the black-painted brick as he lit a cigarette. A tall crown of spikes moved across his head, the most impressive mohawk Silva had ever seen, not that she could say that she'd seen many. His fern green skin glowed under the overhead light, and he was shirtless beneath the black leather jacket he wore. His abdomen was taut beneath the black leather and Silva eyed him appreciatively, her eyes following the dark trail of hair that started at his navel until it disappeared into his tight leather pants.

Heat bloomed to the tips of her long ears when she pulled her gaze from the leather-encased bulge, raising her eyes to meet the tall, punkish orc's. The light over the doorway made the numerous piercings in his pointed ears gleam, the smile that spread across his face, having watched her look him over, was amused and knowing. she dropped her head before quickly yanking the door open, putting distance between herself and further temptation.

Just as they had the previous night, several heads raised as she entered. A beefy fellow near the pool tables gave her a wolfish smile, taking two long strides in her direction before the bartender, the same from the previous evening, called out something in Orcish that made the big orc stop short. Silva felt as if a spotlight had flickered on over her head as several more sets of eyes raised in her direction at the barkeep's guttural words: long looks and suspicious eyes, making her shiver. Scowling, the brawny orc gave her one last sidelong glare before rejoining his friends, and the moment passed.

The bartender was already pouring a glass of the sweet golden alcohol as she approached meekly, hoisting herself onto a stool at the corner as gracefully as she could, rebuffing her in his rough voice as she reached into her small clutch.

"Your money's no good here, beauty," he rasped, setting the glass before her and waving away her attempt to pay. "He'd have my head."

She sipped her drink slowly, somewhat discomfited by the grizzled orc's words, watching the crowd grow as she waited. The bar was packed and noisy, double the crowd from the previous night and Silva noticed that the same bartender seemed to have no problem taking payment from the several groups of women who'd come in—other *sightseers*, from the look of their revealing dresses. Her white sundress was out of place in comparison, but a lady didn't need to advertise, she thought primly, sliding from the stool carefully before picking up the fresh glass that had been placed before her.

It was then that she saw her. At the pool table nearest the wall stood a tall orc woman, towering and muscular, covered in tattoos. Her skin was the color of soft green moss in the spring, a pristine canvas for the dozens of colorful tattoos that snaked up her seemingly endless legs. While just about every orc Silva had encountered wore their hair long, the orc woman had her black hair chopped short, shaved up at the back and sides, letting her long, purple bangs flop appealingly over her heavily-lined eye. The look she leveled on Silva was hungry, and her smile rakish.

Silva watched, transfixed as the intriguing orc bent over the pool table to line up a shot, giving the elf a clear view of her tattooed back and heart-shaped behind, encased in the shortest, tightest denim cut-offs Silva had ever seen, yet somehow they were still *entirely* too much fabric. When the orc woman rose, she could see the tattoos continue into her black crop top, could see them ribboning down her long, well-muscled arms.

There had been a night, during that year after university—when she'd traveled overseas to study Elvish and do volunteer work, preparing her for a lifetime of community service—when dinner had turned to drinks and laughter, and the glamorous elf across the table had given her that same look. The whole point of the trip was to gain some worldly experience and mingle with other well-bred elves in her social strata, she'd told herself at the time, coming home with at least the knowledge of how soft another woman's lips could be.

She found herself now trapped in the orc's salacious gaze, unable to make her feet move or her head turn, and heat moved up her neck as she felt the weight of the woman's eyes drag down her body. A familiar ripple of nerves moved down her spine as the orc approached.

"You look lost, little lamb."

Her voice had a huskiness to it; a deep, bourbon-and-cigarettes voice with an accent like Tate's, and Silva smiled, feeling an odd sense of déjà vu.

"Not lost. Just...deciding."

She could feel the heat from the orc's breath against her neck as she leaned down; heard herself gasp as a hot tongue flicked against her earlobe.

"Well, decide soon, lamby. You look good enough to eat, and I'm positively ravenous."

♥♥♥

Lurielle gripped the table edge, desperately attempting to catch her breath. She couldn't remember an occasion where she'd laughed this much, other than the previous night in the thermae with the same company.

"And then there he was, sitting on the stoop like he'd been waiting for me all night. Seven blocks with split pants and an empty ice cream cone, dragging a leash with no dog attached to it, and he thought he was going to get belly rubs for being such a good boy."

"And I'll bet that's exactly what you did," she wheezed, trying to imagine the gorgeous, smiling orc across from her trudging home with his boxers on display for the block and burst into a fresh round of giggles as she did so.

"Of course that's what I did. Seven blocks and he knew how to get home all by himself! That *is* a good boy."

She had asked how long Khash had his dog, prompting a stream of stories about the hijinks he and the big mastiff had together before he asked about her Yorkie.

"I'm assuming your little bunny rabbit wears tutus and sleeps in a princess bed? Is Lilypiddles her birth name or did she come to you with something even sweeter?"

His smile was wide and his eyes danced with mirth, and Lurielle stole a pepper off his plate in retaliation. The bands of silver around his thick tusks gleamed in the soft glow of the tea light candle on the table, and she felt her heart flutter again at the thought of how handsome he was.

"I'll have you know she's a bonafide killer. There was a nest of squirrels in our front yard and terrorizing them was her favorite thing to do for an entire summer. It got so bad that they ended up having to move, and now I'm paying for their therapy bills. And her name is Junie, for your information."

It had been, once more, the nicest date she'd ever been on, a fact which dismayed as much as it delighted. He had indeed ordered the steak, insisting on her getting a cheese plate to nibble on before they shared dessert. *A man who lets you eat cheese, encourages it even! This really is the dream!* She found it was easy to push Tev's disapproving cluck and her mother's harrumph out of her head with Khash, another check in his favor.

"I like to think my ancestors are all standing around cheering every time I order a steak for dinner that I didn't have to kill with my bare hands," he confided once the amused server had left their table. "Wait...elves...are you a vegetarian?" She laughed as he dropped his head back with a groan. "You should have said something, I can cancel that."

"It doesn't bother me at all," she assured him with a smile. "My boss is a reptilian and he brings in a plastic container of raw meat every day for lunch, and eats it with a cocktail fork."

He asked more about her career, holding his heart and pretending to swoon when she admitted she was an engineer. Lurielle didn't often talk about work; people made awkward assumptions about women in STEM positions, and she'd demurred about exactly what it

was she did the previous evening, only mentioning that she was here with three work friends. Khash only opined that she had beauty *and* brains, and that they clearly had power couple potential. She choked on her wine at his words, relieved that he was placing their dessert order at the time. *Just a piece of meat, just a piece of meat...*

When the decadent looking berries and molten cake were delivered to the table, he insisted she take the first bite, cutting into the gooey cake to let the thick, syrupy center flow out. "This is sinful," she sighed, letting the chocolate melt on her tongue. "A+ ordering skills, sir."

"It's not the only sinful thing..."

His thick, drawling voice made her shiver as his big head lowered to hers. His tongue seemed to move in slow motion as he licked the corner of her mouth, catching a trace of chocolate there before capturing her lower lip between his teeth, sucking slowly. "Mmm...this might be my new favorite way to eat chocolate."

They had been feeding each other bits of the rich cake, with Khash's forkfuls deliberately bumping her lips, giving him a reason to lean down to lick and nibble the chocolate from her mouth, when Lurielle realized she'd be leaving the next day, back to her humdrum life, away from this, away from him and the way he made her feel. Khash took the forkful she held out to him slowly, savoring it with an exaggerated sigh and she giggled again. *Handsome, successful, and funny,* she thought, not for the first time. If he were an elf and she actually spoke to her family about such things, her mother would already be planning the wedding.

"And what do your ancestors think about dessert?" He'd placed his big hand at the back of her chair some time ago, and she shivered at the whisper-soft touch of his fingers at the back of her neck.

"Oh, it is a cacophony in here, darlin'. They are *ecstatic*. 'He got the porterhouse, the chocolate cake, *and* the pretty girl?!' The horn of Grunush is being blown in our honor, Bluebell."

She didn't know what the horn of Grunush was, but as he leaned down to kiss her again, forgetting that it hadn't been her bite, Lurielle was certain she could it hear as well, rattling through the dark restaurant, as loud as her heartbeat.

♥♥♥

The air had already been thick with smoke when she'd finally made it down to the field where the bonfire party was taking place. Ris was surprised by the open landscape, having envisioned the bacchanal taking place somewhere more secluded, like the Ostara festival she'd attended a few years earlier. Held in a clearing in the Applethorpe Wood, she'd not expected *that* observance to end in an orgiastic revel, but had enthusiastically joined in the celebration, despite barely knowing anything about human witchcraft at the time, finding herself being taken by a satyr she thought she'd recognized from the grocery store.

The field housing the orcs' bonfire party, by contrast, was open on all sides, overlooking the scenic valley and ringed in pedestrian

footpaths. *They don't care about privacy, obviously. Although it's not like anyone here has much to hide...* She could see the outline of bodies against the indigo skyline already pressed together in compromising positions, her eyes following the movement of one orc's thrusting hips as she neared the fire. *They don't waste time, either.*

In all the times she and her friends had giggled over visiting the commune and her private suppositions over what the experience might be like, her imagination had never accounted for the presence of other women crowding the scene, there for the same thing.

Instead, she'd imagined a bevy of sexy, handsome orcs, all lining up to lavish her with attention. She'd pictured one kissing her feet, another moving his hands over her small breasts, while a third knelt between her open legs, pleasuring her with his tongue, the others patiently waiting their turn...she could see immediately that those daydreams were rooted in pure fantasy. The number of other sightseers scattered through the grass had not been accounted for in her imagination, nor had the greed of the men involved in the situation.

She watched a tall, muscular form striding up to a circle of his fellows, his erection bouncing with every step, stroking himself as he waited for the circle to open to receive him. As Ris moved closer, she saw what it was he waited for: two goblins knelt in the grass, their full breasts heaving as they gasped for air, taking turns as they orally serviced the orcs around them. As one orc finished, another took his place, a never-ending circle for the girls, and Ris shuddered. She was hardly naive and knew species mattered little when lust clouded judgment, and she certainly couldn't judge the goblins: her raison d'etre for the weekend was to be the filling in an orc sandwich after all. Still, the gap between her imagination and reality was startling. *Time to get your head in the game if you want to go home bow-legged.*

There was no sign of her handsome poet from that morning, regrettably, but as she scanned the crowd, she spotted the orc from the previous evening, who'd invited her to the bonfire. He'd chuckled when she had appeared before him in the resort's lawn, asking where she was running off to at such a late hour. She wanted to meet someone who respected her, who held her interest and excited more than just her body...but she knew how to handle men who were only looking for one thing. The orc had grunted in pleased surprise when she'd trailed the tip of her long nail down the dark trail of hair at his navel. Up and down, up and down, she made several passes over his skin before his cock had responded, and she'd dropped to her knees, the shadow of their balcony providing scant cover as she knelt in the grass.

Now he stood on the opposite side of the massive fire pit, watching a curvaceous hulder being taken by an orc with stone-colored skin. There was a cluster of other sightseers, Ris saw as she approached: hanging back, working up the nerve to take the plunge. She wondered if they too were finding the reality of the situation a far cry from their fantasies, but decided that was *their* issue to grapple with. *She* was going home with a story to tell. She wasn't sure if the

orc even recognized her as she placed herself in his line of vision, but he'd reached out to take her outstretched hand all the same. *Just a piece of meat.* Lurielle's question from that morning floated back to her as she found herself impaled on his giant cock a very short time later—she'd never learned his name, and if he'd told her, she didn't remember. *What does it matter?* His chest was broad, his skin a deep forest green, and his cock was thick enough that she'd felt the burn of his entry, despite her arousal. *What more do I need to know?*

♥♥♥

She tasted like the amber-colored alcohol she drank: a sharp edge with hints of vanilla. Elshona was her name, and her hands seemed to be everywhere, as they reclined on one of the sofas in the little back room. Silva learned she was a chef, had lived in the village for several years, and that she was divorced, which was *deeply* frowned upon in Orcish culture, evidently.

"We were friends growing up," she'd shrugged, swallowing another mouthful of the dark amber drink. "He did all of my tattoos, has himself a little shop in the town we're from. It was just...a bad decision. On both our parts. But that's why I'm here, so. When you're an outcast, you find other outcasts."

Silva didn't stop her when Elshona leaned down to kiss her, enjoying the slight scrape of tusks and the feeling of hugely muscled arms when she'd pulled the much smaller elf to her lap.

"Soft as satin," the orc whispered against her skin, lips trailing down her lavender neck and over the tops of her breasts. She was so distracted by the pressure of Elshona's tongue ring moving against the inside of her mouth that she scarcely felt the hand that slipped beneath the hem of her dress, not until fingers lightly caressed the front of her dampened panties, making her jump.

"Are you sensitive there, little lamby?" Fingertips stroked against the pink lace again, and again and again, until Silva gasped against her lips, wanting *more*. "Mmm, I think you're *very* sensitive there."

She made no resistance when the kiss deepened, hungry and demanding, nor when a finger slipped beneath the edge of the lace,

gliding through her folds to rest at that little bundle of nerves that made her squirm against the bigger woman's hand. She arched into the delicious pressure of that wide fingertip against her clit, and when it began to circle lightly, Silva whimpered against Elshona's mouth.

"You even make noises like a little lamb. Already so wet...I can make this little kitty of yours purr...would you like that?"

Silva bleated in pleasure and need, the room spinning as long fingers continued stroking her, dipping into her until Elshona asked if her friends out in the bar were going to come looking for her. "I-I'm here alone," she gasped, pressing herself against the caressing digits, seeking more contact. "I was waiting...Tate...I was waiting for a guy I met yesterday..."

Almost instantly, the finger that had been rubbing pleasurably at her clit pulled back, as well as Elshona's kiss. "Tate? You're not with those girls at the bar? You're *Tate's?*"

Elshona leaned back even further, looking Silva over as though there might have been a lighted placard around her neck, one that she'd missed in her hurry to get into the adorable elf's delicate underthings. The orc's eyes narrowed in consternation as she retrieved her phone from the back pocket of her skin-tight shorts.

"Oi...you headin' to the Pixie? I have a little lamb here, says she belongs to you, pretty little elf...'m I allowed to play with her?"

Silva twisted in frustration, desperately hoping the answer was *yes* as she squirmed against the orc woman's lap. She wasn't entirely sure how she felt about being labeled as someone's property; she should have been wildly offended, she was sure. Instead, it sent a tremor of excitement up her back when she belatedly realized whom Elshona had called. Tate was on the phone, *her* Tate, possibly on his way there right that moment! She bit her lip, wondering what he would think, if he'd be disgusted. She had a feeling the situation would make that sharp smile gleam, but she wasn't positive...

Silva watched Elshona's eyes narrow before widening comically, looking Silva over with a scrunched brow. "Yes, pretty little elf, like I said. I mean, yes, *obviously* that's what I mean...yes! With her! Have you gone daft? Why do I need to keep repeating myself? Why are you laughing?!"

Silva could hear Tate's musical laughter through the phone and felt her own smile grow, able to clearly picture his crowded grin.

"Oh...you want to do *that*? I'm not sure she'll be...if you think so... fine, I'll keep her warmed up 'til you finish, then." Her eyes rolled dramatically before she huffed. "Fine, she's a dove, not a lamb. Don't dawdle, you can finish counting in the morning."

The look Elshona leveled upon her was speculative, and Silva fidgeted impatiently as the tall orc slid her phone into the back pocket of her tight shorts. "Well, he said I get to play with you, lamby...but he wants to watch. He'll be round soon as he's finished with inventory. A real stickler for the rules, that one, 'specially if they're his. But," she paused, giving Silva the same rapacious stare she had over the pool table, pulling Silva to straddle her muscular thighs, "that doesn't mean we can't have a bit of fun before he comes down."

Elshona's fingers once more traced over the top of the pink lace, teasing at the apex of her sex until Silva moaned in frustration, bouncing against the other woman's lap to find the friction she'd craved. "I think I want to have a taste of you first. Would you like that lamby? If I lick that perfect little kitty will you be a good lamb and come on my tongue for me?"

Silva was unable to remember if she'd ever enjoyed playing the submissive this much before, deciding that her needy little whine of agreement was worth it when her panties were slid down her narrow hips and stuffed into the back pocket of the grinning orc's shorts, those long fingers dragged through her wet folds once more.

Elshona wasted no time before pushing her back and licking a hot stripe over her slick center. The orc's wide tongue circled and teased around the spot where she *needed* attention until Silva keened, begging for more contact, nearly crying in relief when at last Elshona puckered her lips to suck on the throbbing little pearl. She alternated passes of her tongue with soft little suckles, growing in their intensity until Silva was bucking her hips against the orc's mouth, *desperate*, desperate for release.

She begged. She wasn't sure if it was something she'd done before, knew it absolutely wasn't proper, but she was having fun, wasn't she? Silva of the night time didn't need to worry about propriety, after all, and begging to come simply seemed like the right thing to do.

Her plot worked, a direly needed victory. Elshona cooed about her being a good little lamb before fastening her lips, nursing on the swollen, throbbing bundle of nerves, sucking her clit steadily until Silva arched, legs shaking. She felt the vibrations of Elshona's throaty moan against her as she came, pulsing against the other woman's tongue as it continued to lap against her, until she was boneless and spent, and the orc's face glistened.

Over Elshona's shoulder, leaning in the doorway, Tate's smile was wider than she'd ever seen it, stretched back to his ears. His teeth were like daggers, longer than Silva remembered them being just that morning, and his mirth-filled eyes held hers without blinking.

"If you've got a tab, go settle it."

Elshona rose quickly, ducking from the room as he approached the sofa where she sprawled, still pulsing from her orgasm. He moved like a cat, Silva thought, lithe and silent, lowering his head to dip his tongue between her hot folds, tasting her release before crawling up her body.

"You've been having all sorts of adventures without me, dove," he murmured, gripping her chin before leaning in slowly. His mouth was still sweet, she thought, although she tasted herself there as well.

He was smaller than the other orcs, lean where they were bulky, but Silva was reminded that he was still much bigger than her when he lifted her like a doll, carrying her across the room to a closed door she hadn't previously noticed. She tightened her legs around his waist when they ascended a pitch-black staircase, burying her face in his neck to breathe in the heady sandalwood smell of him, hoping she would get to feel the drag of those teeth on her skin before morning.

♥♥♥

"I'm sorry that I'm keeping you from your pantless time," she'd murmured as he'd kissed her after they left the restaurant. The little cobblestone alleyway was lit with twinkle lights, strung across the road every few feet, giving the the lane an ethereal, cozy glow under the inky-black sky. Khash had pulled her to a curved-back bench to kiss her silly, and she clung to his collar panting when they, at last, came up for air.

"Oh, I'd say this was well worth it," he chuckled. "Do I need to get you back to your room before your friends get worried? I wouldn't want you to turn into a pumpkin on me."

"My friends probably don't even realize I'm gone. Ris was heading to some bonfire party and I don't even know where Silva was heading...everyone was pretty eager to go their own way after dinner." She'd been counting on being able to keep her head down and listen with half an ear to her friend's chatter over dinner, but Ris had shifted impatiently in her red bandage dress, checking the time on her phone and tapping a long nail against the side of her water glass, while Silva's attention had been fixed unwaveringly on the bistro across the intersection. All three had been distracted and had gone their separate ways with very little conversation as they left the restaurant. "I definitely don't have any reason to rush back."

"Well, it's a fine night for strollin'," he grinned down with his crinkled eyes and dimpled chin and Lurielle wondered how she was meant to go back to her Khash-less life on Monday, "and pantless time can still be found."

Strolling led to walking the entire length of the little downtown, and back past the resort grounds. Lurielle relished the heat from his big body beside her, her arm wrapped around his meaty forearm as they walked. Along the way, Khash had turned the conversation into a game of *Pantless Time with Bluebell*, as he called it, trying to determine what she was willing to do naked.

"Do you swim?" he'd asked hopefully, pointing out that the shimmering lake wasn't far.

"You can see that lake from the road!" she exclaimed with an indignant laugh. "As a matter of fact, we saw this huge, naked orc coming out of the water when we pulled up—big dog, sexy accent, works in finance, maybe you know him?—and he waggled his junk at us!"

Lurielle loved the way his shoulders shook when he laughed, the way his ears flushed dark as he wheezed, the way his entire face smiled, and especially the way he tightened his arm around hers as he recovered.

"I have absolutely no idea what you're talkin' about. I do not *waggle*."

He conceded that the lake water might be too cold for "her delicate little petals" now that it was nighttime, and she absolutely refused to go naked horseback riding. They had circled the entire Main Street by then, and were passing a black-bricked tavern when several shrieking women tumbled out of the door. Lurielle immediately recognized the drunken harpy from the tiki bar the night before.

"What time are the fireworks?" one of the girls asked another, and Lurielle turned up to Khash with a smile as the trio of women giggled their way down the sidewalk.

"Are there fireworks? That sounds nice...can we go someplace private to watch?"

They would go back to his place, it was decided, because she was not willing to walk all the way down from the resort without her clothes, and then venture to what Khash claimed was "the perfect spot" to watch the fireworks from the other side of the lake. Lurielle could feel her breath getting shorter with every step as they set off for his cabin, giddy adrenaline mixed with gut churning fear that she was actually going to let this sexy, syrupy-voiced orc talk her into showing her dimpled thighs and sagging breasts to the world.

It's dark out, there's not going to be anyone around anyways, she tried to convince herself. No one would see. ...*He* would see though, and that was possibly the worst part of it, he would see her: jiggling ass and too-eager eyes, someone he could have a weekend fling with, but certainly not good enough to date, not for someone like him, handsome and charming as he was. They passed by the aforementioned lake as her thoughts continued to spiral, her confidence dimming with every step.

There were fish in the lake, Khash said, squeezing her arm and distracting her from her panic, and he opined that some of them might be big enough to swallow her whole. "But the little ones will just nibble your toes, and we can pretend we're at one of those fancy spas. Next time, maybe..."

She nearly choked in laughter, even as her heart twisted. *Next time...* She wished there could be a next time, wished for the hundredth time that she had met him on Dynah's dating app, that he wasn't the byproduct of a weekend meant for meaningless hookups.

"It's a good lake for fishin'," he mused, oblivious to her inner turmoil. "I like to come early, when all the partiers are still sleeping off their night."

"I used to go fishing with my granddad when I was little," she confided, tightening her arm around his, easily able to picture his big silhouette against the early morning sun at the lake's edge. "I loved it. My mom was worried I would turn into a tomboy and only let him take my brother after I started school."

He harrumphed to himself before tugging her closer. "Me too. Granddaddy would take the lot of us, plus my cousins. Twelve kids, and he had us lined up like soldiers. Worked his fingers to the bone so that each one of us could go to good schools, be better than the generation before. Used to sit me on his knee and let me count his money, over and over again, addin' it up, subtracting, dividing. Never was much of it, but I had the best math grades in my class every year."

"My mom wanted me to major in Art History." Lurielle wrinkled her nose at the memory as Khash chuckled. "She was furious with me when I did engineering. Then I met my boyfriend at the end of my first year, and she decided school was just a means to an end anyway and it didn't matter what I studied."

"And look at us now," he drawled, pulling her to a stop, wrapping his arms around her. "Good jobs doing things we enjoy, eating

chocolate cake and enjoying pantless fireworks. I don't have any complaints, do you?"

She squeaked when he lifted her, as he'd done the previous night, and gripped his neck tightly as he kissed her. "Not a single one."

His cabin was set back from the path, backing up to a small stream, and she understood why he found it peaceful. The moment of truth came before she was fully ready for it, but nevertheless, she shimmied out of her dress in his small bathroom, folding it carefully, placing her bra and panties between the folds.

You're not really going to go through with this, are you? Completely naked, outside? Maybe if you'd joined that spin class... Lurielle pushed her ex's voice aside with an annoyed grunt. "As a matter of fact, I *am*," she hissed at her reflection in the bathroom mirror. She'd never done anything like this, and it was fine to be nervous, she assured herself, buoyed by her irritation at Tev's continued presence in her head.

She'd done all sorts of new things since being one her own... she'd bought her house, got a dog, joined a group that went hiking through the Metroparks every third Sunday. She'd learned every nook and cranny of her new town, quaint as it was, and most of that she'd done completely on her own. She'd gone ziplining with Ris and Dynah at some farm, a completely terrifying experience, and slightly humiliating because there were weight restrictions on the lines, and she'd had to make sure she wasn't zooming down one that would plummet her to her death, but still—she'd done it, had a good time, had even been hit on by some guy, a brawny minotaur. She was happy with her life and happy with herself, mostly, and she didn't need to let the harsh critics of her past continue to drag her down.

She was not at all ready, but that was as ready as she'd ever be, Lurielle decided, creaking the door open with her heart in her mouth. The only light that showed was from the open front door, where Khash stood waiting patiently for her. Her heart stuck in throat as she gulped at the sight of him. He seemed slimmer without clothes, with his broad back and muscular arms unconfined. His full ass was perfectly rounded in the moonlight, leading to long, thick thighs. Khash seemed completely at ease, rolling one of his shoulders in the warm night air with a rolled up blanket under his arm, and when she stepped through the doorway, he turned with that lazy smile.

"Just pull that shut, darlin'. Let's go find us our perfect spot."

Silva felt as though she were on a carnival ride. There had been a fair at one of the local farms the summer prior, and her date had dragged her onto the Spinning Vortex ride several times in a row, oblivious to the way she staggered, unable to keep the world from tilting and whirling.

It was how she felt now, as her hand curled tightly around the cue ball. Tate's teeth were like needles dragging over her ankle, pressing to her skin as his cock pressed into her body, his teeth gentling just before he broke the skin, hilting in her fully, and Silva gasped at the sensation.

The apartment above the bar was huge, spanning the length of the entire building with giant windows overlooking the street beyond. She'd been able to see the twinkling lane below earlier, when she'd sat astride Elshona's hips, watching a constant stream of orcs and the tourists they'd met moving up and down the block. She'd never experienced the sensation of her bare sex sliding against another woman's, but with every slow pump of Tate's hips behind her, her clit rubbed into Elshona's, and both women had cried out.

Then she'd been spun, her thighs straddling the orc woman's face, feeling that hot tongue slide into her once more. She'd never tasted another woman before, had never put her lips and tongue to silky-slick folds, but decided she wanted to try. Silva leaned down to give an experimental lick, then another, gripping Elshona's muscular thighs for support. Tangy, certainly not unpleasant, and when she moved her tongue against that hooded pearl, she felt the reverberation of the bigger woman's moan.

The pre-come soaked tip of Tate's cock had been pressed to her lips next, slippery and sweet, pushing into her mouth until her jaw screamed in protest. She wanted to taste him, wanted him to make good on his promise of filling her mouth, but he held her hair tightly, controlling her movement, and pulled back every time she'd started to gag. Silva had lost count of how many times she'd climaxed by the time she'd been placed on the pool table.

The low lights of the apartment's corners had been dimmed further, bathing the room in a pink glow as she stared up at the tall ceiling. Pressed tin tiles, she noted, giving the space a unique, vintage feel. Whoever had done the interior work truly had a wonderful eye for detail, she thought, as Tate pulled her legs to his shoulders and her bottom flush to the edge of the table, lining his cock up to her entrance.

Elshona had already begged off any more. Too over-sensitized, she said, too tired, starting to get a crick in her neck. Wondered aloud if her boss was going to give her the morning off, seeing how late it was already. Tate removed his teeth from Silva's ankle long enough to singsong something in a language she didn't understand, to which Elshona huffed. He smiled that malevolent smile, which Silva returned as widely as she was able, and then his teeth found her foot again; her ankle, her calf. When he released her legs to lean forward, covering her body with his own, she gasped, every bit of air in her lungs leaving in a great *whoosh*. She had thought he was fully hilted in her already, but this flush angle gave new meaning to *fullness*, and she cried out

again and again with every unhurried thrust. His topknot had long ago begun to unwind, leaving silky strands of his glossy black hair loose around his long, slender neck, and Silva wrapped her fingers through the unconstrained hair as his teeth dragged at her throat, holding him there. She *wanted* to be bitten.

"You should come home with me, dove," he whispered instead, teeth needling into her earlobe and scraping the side of her neck. "Step through the clover and put all of that expectation behind you."

She didn't know how it was that he seemed to be in her head, knowing her thoughts, and she tightened her legs around him in response. His hips were now a relentless hammer against hers, the cue ball a terrible thing to grip for support, and his whisper an insidious current in her ear. Silva of the daylight hours knew one couldn't trust the fae, that their promises were false and all their words poisoned, but, she reminded herself, he was Elvish too, and Orcish, and Silva of the nighttime wanted to believe his promises.

Her limbs trembled and her head spun, the shiny-smooth ball in her hand rattling against the table's felted surface. Despite the fact she and Elshona both were rung out from an overabundance of pleasure, Tate's movements had been slow and languorous all night—leisurely, shallow pumps, never climaxing; more watching than participation, but now Silva felt the urgency in his hips, the snap of his jaws as his teeth found her throat and shoulders.

She clenched around him with a gasp for a final time when his dagger teeth broke her lavender skin at last, crying out as her back arched off the green felt. The cue ball rolled across the table, out of her grasp as she spasmed, feeling Tate's spine ripple with his own release above her. Slow and languorous again, as he'd been the whole night, drawing out his pleasure with her in long spurts. Hot tongue replaced sharp teeth, as he slumped in her arms, laving at the blood that welled where he'd bitten her. The room pitched and her head swam, and all she was cognizant of was Tate's lips and Tate's voice, softly kissing her chin, her nose, the spot where he'd bitten her, calling her his Silva of the nighttime.

♥♥♥

The smoke and noise from the bonfire bled through the trees as they walked. The trail had been quiet until then, and with every step, she tried to convince herself that she was more comfortable being naked out in the open air. At least, until two large bodies appeared before them: two orcs, making their way up the trail slowly. The men were similarly unclothed and deep in conversation and paid her and Khash little mind as they passed.

The bubble of panic that had grown in her chest as the orcs had drawn nearer dissolved into a giddy heat at the way they'd barely looked askance at her jiggling thighs and untoned arms; a giddiness that carried her up the hill on weightless feet, that had her squeezing Khash's giant hand, his fingers laced with her own. Her heart was a timpani when she gingerly lowered herself to the thick quilt he'd spread on the grass, attempting to be as graceful as possible. The sky was a wide-open canopy of stars above them, reminding her of the old observatory at home that she'd been to once, but the stars held little interest when compared with the big orc beside her.

Khash's voice was a heavy slur, pooling around her in the warm night air, and Lurielle was certain that whatever he was saying was probably funny and clever, because it always seemed to be, but she didn't hear a single word of it. Adrenaline raced through her veins, and all she wanted to do was kiss him. Her hand looked tiny in the center of his broad chest, as she sat up slowly, turning to face him. His heavy-lidded gaze set her blood to a slow simmer, much like the steamy water of the thermae the previous night, that slow, lazy smile stretching his mouth. She was barely aware of the fact that she'd lowered herself to him, not until his big hand cupped the back of her head as their mouths met.

His full lips were softest, sweetest thing she'd ever tasted, and she wondered again how she was supposed to return to the real world the next afternoon, putting this weekend behind.

You were supposed to be here having fun, stupid. Drink champagne with your friends, get laid, not go falling for someone. They'd done the first part, she considered, thinking of the outsized bottle of champagne the handsome, creepy server at the bistro had foisted upon them. Lurielle could see no reason why she couldn't make the second part a reality. The fact that she was falling for him could be put aside for the moment, she encouraged herself. It would hurt worse in the morning, maybe, but right now...right now she felt brave and beautiful, and there was no time like the present.

His skin was warm as she slid her palm over his chest, circling his nipple until it pebbled beneath her thumb. From her vantage point, she was able to look down the long expanse of his body and watch as his cock slowly inflated, the way it twitched when she gave the same nipple a pinch and rubbed circles against his stomach. It jerked against his thigh when her fingertips traced down that dark trail of hair from his navel, and his breath stuttered against her lips when she paused to kiss him.

"We don't need to...we don't have to do anything you don't want to, Lurielle..." His voice was once more a slow spill of amber honey,

tripping over itself before clinging to and coating every letter of her name, making it sound like something beautiful and desirable; nothing that she was, but it was the way he made her feel. She smiled widely as he grunted, her nails tracing back up his body to scratch lightly at his throat.

"Oh, I don't *need* to do anything," she agreed after a moment, slowly sliding her fingers back down his stomach, feeling his muscles bunch and dance beneath her palm. His thick cock jerked against her hand as she gripped it, giving it a slow pump. "But I *want* to. Doesn't that make a difference? Are we both consenting adults, Khash?"

His lazy smile quickened her breath, and she tightened her grip in response. "Far be it from me to keep a lady from her heart's truest desires. And yes, we most certainly are."

She loved the noises he made as she stroked him, loved the way his moans vibrated against her lips, loved the staccato of his thundering heartbeat as she kissed her way down his body.

There was already a pearl of pre-come welling at his tip when her tongue smoothed over it, licking it away before swirling over the shiny, dark green head. She could hear his breaths getting heavier as she sucked him beneath the stars, heard his little moans and grunts interspersed with muttered curses as his balls contracted, his hand tightening in her hair as her jaw ached.

Her eyes streamed as his hand tightened in her hair, a dull fire blooming in her jaw. Lurielle didn't understand how he could be so thick, how it was even possible to fit that much girth into his well-tailored pants, how it was even fair for him to be charming and handsome, successful and funny, and still have such a perfect cock. Most men would be happy with one or two, she thought as she pulled back for a breath, sucking the underside of his swollen head as she did so.

Khash's moan of pleasure was as thick and syrupy as his speaking voice, and she sucked the spot again, hoping to elicit the same sound from his throat.

"Darlin', you keep that up and I'll be taking you home to meet mama tonight," he groaned, fisting her unruly hair.

She choked when he made the comment about bringing her home, taking more than she could comfortably swallow and she pulled back with a gag.

The pressure against her scalp loosened then, and he urged her to sit up, panting. "You're trying to kill me, Bluebell," he laughed weakly between his heavy breaths.

She could practically see the shape of him pulsing in the darkness, knew it wouldn't take much more to make him come. "Then let me finish what I started, you big dummy." Then at least they'd be even.

"No...that's not the way I want to finish, darlin'..."

His kiss was a bit rougher when she crashed her lips to his, feeling a shiver move down to her toes as his hands moved over her—tracing the shape of her breasts, cupping her hips, squeezing her thighs. Straddling his body was like climbing onto a horse, wide and firm, and Lurielle was certain he must have been able to hear the crash of

her heartbeat as she swung her leg awkwardly across his hips. She was barely able to keep both knees on the ground at the same time, bracing herself against his chest.

The downside to pantsless time, she realized, was that the orc-sized condoms in her clutch were back at his cabin, with her dress. But, she rationalized, as she guided his thick length to her entrance, she was on birth control and she'd never been irresponsible before. If all this weekend was meant to be was a meaningless fling, then by goddess, she was getting the fling out of it.

Her gasp was swallowed by a pop in the air, followed by the first shimmer of sparks in the sky overhead, his girth far greater than anything she'd experienced before. Khash captured the stiffened peak of her breast between his lips, groaning against her skin as she cried out, pressing down on him slowly. It didn't matter then, as she arched her back, impaled upon him, that she was self-conscious and awkward. The jiggliness of her ass didn't seem important as he gripped it tightly, squeezing as her hips rolled; the heaviness of her breasts inconsequential as he groaned against them.

The only thing that mattered was his hips, rising to meet hers urgently; his hands, gripping her firmly, and the only thing she could hear, above the cacophonous din above their heads—Khash's voice, murmuring her name, over and over again, making it sound exotic and luxurious; leaning on the *Ls* and tugging on the vowels, not at all sounding like a man having a meaningless fling, she convinced herself. It would hurt tomorrow when she said goodbye. But tomorrow was tomorrow, and she was done being afraid of tomorrows.

His fingers had begun to circle into her, helping her to catch up with his ardor, and it didn't take long for her to feel that rising crest of release, a great wave of pleasure that threatened to swallow her up in its intensity. Khash's deep moan was swallowed by a sonic boom and another release of shimmering gold sparks as he jerked against her, and the feeling of his liquid heat spreading through her was enough to tip her over the edge, tightening around him. Lurielle let her head drop back as her clenching contractions released another stream of worshipful curses from his lips, the fireworks around them mirroring the fireworks in her mind. Above her head, the sky was a brilliant explosion of color, and she had never felt more beautiful.

Her head was heavy when he pulled out of her carefully, the big room spinning. She felt the brief touch of his lips to hers, and then she was cold, exposed to the open room. Silva watched him through her heavy, hooded eyes as he gingerly removed the sodden condom before disappearing into the darkness of the hallway.

"Lock up on your way out," she heard him tell Elshona, who was half-dressed and half-asleep, laying on the sofa opposite where Silva carefully sat up.

Tate did not return.

"Do you need a lift, lamby?"

It took her a moment to realize that she was the lamb in question, and that the big orc woman now stood before her, fully dressed. Elshona paused in lacing up her boots, cocking an expectant eyebrow in wait. Did she? Silva couldn't imagine walking home in her condition, she felt well-used and weak, but she wasn't sure if she was being left a choice, and the thought made her stomach lurch.

She knew that if she left with the beautiful orc woman, she would start to cry, and if she started to cry, she wouldn't be able to stop, and didn't relish the idea of ending the night that way. She'd likely cry anyways, but at least she could take her time, staggering through the darkness alone.

"Well, I'm off then. Be careful, lamby, don't go wandering too close to the cabins." She felt the heat of the taller woman when she bent down to press her full lips to Silva's forehead, and then she was gone too, leaving her alone in the big room.

Her dress was in the bedroom, she remembered, walking unsteadily through the darkened hallway. The street beyond was deserted, the twinkle lights off, and all the bars and restaurants closed. She didn't especially like the dark, never had, not since childhood; too afraid of the unknown things lurking in the shadows. It would be a scary walk back to the resort without his big hand holding hers securely, she realized swallowing thickly, already feeling her face begin to heat.

She wondered if Ris had found her bonfire, if Lurielle had a nice time wherever she was going, looking so pretty. Silva admired Lurielle, though she'd never been brave enough to tell her so. She had walked away from the expectations of her family, had ended a relationship with her perfect, marriage-material Elvish boyfriend, and had moved away to start her own life. Freedom Silva could only dream of. She continued through the dark apartment, deciding she at least wanted to say goodnight, to say goodbye. She wouldn't ever see him again after she walked out those doors, and for some reason the thought made her chest tighten, making it hard to draw breath.

He was in another bedroom, larger, with the biggest bed she'd ever seen, all pristine white sheets and down duvet. Tate was bending over the closet, and she took a moment to admire the long line of his pale green back before he straightened up, two huge, fluffy pillows in hand.

"There's a toothbrush for you, dove, on the sink...do you need anything? Are you hungry?"

She stumbled a bit when he turned towards her, her shaking knees unable or unwilling to hold her up for another moment, not when she felt so confused and uncertain. Tate's arms were around her in the next heartbeat, and then she was across his lap, sitting at the edge of the big bed.

"Are you alright, dove? Did I hurt you?"

Her lungs began to inflate on their own once more as he checked her over with clinical concern, despite her assurance that she was fine, even though she wasn't sure that was entirely true. "Do you want to take a hot bath? Are you sure you don't want food?"

The room still spun as she lifted her head from his shoulder, although perhaps not as badly as it had done a few minutes earlier. "What...what are you going to do?"

His slim eyebrow raised, the dim light of the room making the silver bands there glow. "It's the middle of the night, Silva. I'm going to bed."

"Bed sounds good," she whispered.

The bathroom across the hall was similarly all white, gleaming subway tiles with an ornate antique mirror above the pedestal sink. Silva brushed her teeth, cupping her hand beneath the tap to drink several mouthfuls of the cold water before she hesitantly tiptoed back to the now dark bedroom. Although his teeth gleamed in the moonlight, the smile he gave her was less sharp, softer than what she'd seen from him previously, which she returned with a tremulous smile of her own when he patted the turned-down side of the bed.

Her eyes swept the room when he turned her to unzip her dress, despite the fact that she could have easily pulled it over her head. A large, antique bureau was on the wall across from the bed, with a twin on the wall beside her, Elvish in provenance and very well cared for. The tables on either side of the big bed were similarly styled Elvish antiques, while the bed itself was completely modern, sleek and black, piled high with the fluffy bedding, and she was unable to hold in a little sigh of contentment when he pulled her into the white cocoon beside him. She had grown up in a privileged, insular world and recognized luxury when it was in front of her; these were high thread-count sheets of the best quality, the duvet was filled with fluffy down. She didn't understand how a bartender could afford such finery, but nothing about this weekend had made a particularly great deal of sense.

"Are you sure you're not hungry? Three a.m. colcannon to stick to your bones? I'm a very good cook, I'll have you know."

She laughed as he pulled her to his side, tucking the duvet around them. "No, I'm good." Her head seemed to fit perfectly against the center of his chest, and her breath caught when she felt his lips press lightly to her forehead as his arm settled around her. The long line of his body pressed to hers, warm and solid; the arm he'd folded over her was heavy and secure. She realized she'd be saying goodbye tomorrow, and wasn't able to articulate to herself why the thought upset her as much as it did.

"Sweet dreams, little dove. I wish I could tell you it won't be an early morning, but the Sunday breakfast crowd is madness."

Silva snuggled against him, pushing down the sob she felt brewing in her chest when he tangled his fingers into her hair. He smelled like sandalwood and freedom, and she wondered if she would ever get to know what that was.

♥♥♥

Part 03

♥ The Morning After ♥

The big bed was impossibly comfortable.

Ris jumped as her alarm sounded, buzzing her phone across the nightstand beside her. It had been the middle of the night when she'd staggered back to the resort, peeling off her dress and dropping into bed naked, unable to hold her head up for another moment. The bonfire had been...an experience. She was not sure it was one she'd ever want to repeat, but she could say that she'd done it and had gotten exactly what she'd come looking for.

The orc who'd invited her had taken her kneeling in the thick grass, rutting her like an animal, the exact sort of mindless fucking she'd been expecting all weekend. When the orc who had been watching appreciatively

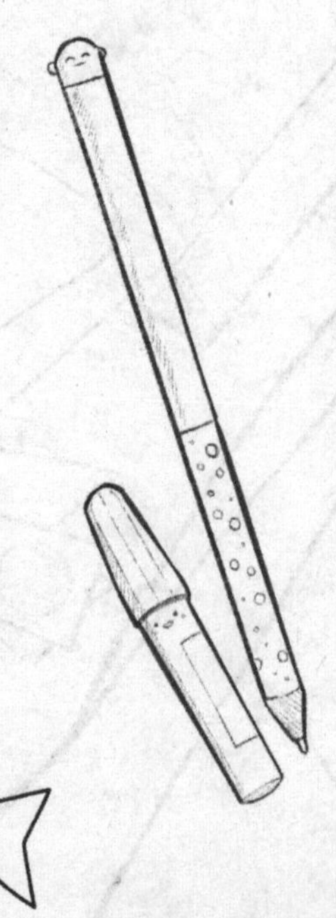

had approached her from the front, smearing the glistening tip of his cock across her lips, Ris had opened her mouth welcomingly, imaging a swirling black line cutting through '*spit-roasted by orcs*' on her sexual bucket list.

The one in the front had been rougher than she'd anticipated. Darkness had closed in on her several times, her airway completely constricted by his thick length, but he'd pulled back each time and she'd wheezed in a lungful of air, drool running down her chest, just before he'd pushed his way into her mouth once more. When the orc behind her orgasmed with a shudder, the thick cock had left her mouth, switching sides to fuck into her from behind, until he too had finished.

She'd been taken again by an ochre-skinned orc with huge tusks and a clan tattoo covering his broad back, pounding into her on the edge of a picnic table, yowling his climax into the sky. The first orc, the one who'd invited her, had already recovered from his peak and had moved on to another girl at that point, an ecstatic harpy. Ris could see her feathered shoulders bouncing as she was held aloft in huge, green arms, and turned away, not needing to see or do anymore. She'd had the experience she'd been seeking, and that was good enough. If she's stayed any longer, she might have sustained an injury, and she'd already felt well-used at that point.

She'd only come twice, she'd realized as she located her dress at the base of a bush, slowly walking through the condom wrapper-strewn grass on shaky legs. The little downtown was dark as she teetered through, her ankles wobbling on the cobblestones, past the little bistro, past the soap maker and the apiarist, past the black-bricked building where the handsome orc had been shouting on the sidewalk. She wondered what Lurielle had gotten up to, dressed as nice as she had been. Silva had, as usual, looked like she'd stepped from the pages of Better Elves Weekly, in a prim white dress and a tulip pink scarf knotted at her neck. She'd probably spent the night in the resort lobby, charming the bellhops and retiring by nine.

She'd dropped into bed in a heap, unconscious as soon as her head hit the pillow. Now the light streamed through her windows, and Ris rolled over with a groan. She was sore, she was probably bruised, and felt as if she could sleep for a week. Despite that, she pulled herself from the bed. They would need to check out soon, and unlike her friends, her belongings had not been kept neatly in her bag.

"Ladies, I'm going to jump in the shower, 'kay?"

Silence greeted her as she stepped from her room, wrapping a towel around her long, slender frame. "Luri? Silva?"

Silva's already-packed quilted bag sat on the end of her still-made bed, and a check to Lurielle's room showed a similarly unslept in bed. She was the only one who'd made it back to the room the previous night.

"Un-fucking-believable..."

The big bed was impossibly comfortable.

Silva stirred, wrinkling her nose as something tickled her, snuggling deeper into her fluffy pillow. She felt as though she were floating in a sea of softness, enveloped between the crisp, cool sheets and thick duvet. She'd wondered about the heavy weight of the bedclothes last night, but she'd been too sleepy, too emotional and heavy after their bacchanal, and far too comfortable in his arms to question it. It wasn't until later, when she'd carefully extracted herself to tiptoe to the bathroom, that she'd felt the arctic gust of air through the vents, raising goosebumps on her arms. Sliding back under the covers with him had been a relief, worming her way back into his embrace. He'd rolled to his side once she'd left the warmth of his arms, but they'd come back around her as soon as she pressed to his front, her nose against his throat and his knee pushing through her legs until they were a tightly pressed tangle of limbs.

Something grazed her nose again, and she twitched, burying her face in the pillow with a whimper. Beside her, Tate chuckled. "Time to rise and shine, dove."

"It's too early," she moaned into the smooth, white cotton. The room was dim with grey, early morning haze, and she felt as though she could easily sleep for hours more.

"You've got the right of it...but I need to open the restaurant. If 'Shona gets in first, I'll never hear the end of things. I'll make you breakfast when we get there."

When she squinted open her eyes, Tate's face was inches from hers, their noses practically touching. Silva realized she'd taken over his pillow sometime in the night, cuddling closer and closer every time she shifted.

"You can't be trusted, you tried to get me drunk at breakfast yesterday," she accused sleepily, earning herself a sharp-toothed grin.

"I'm starting to think it's not possible to do such a thing. We could make that into a tidy sideline," he mused, as Silva snuggled closer, wanting to feel the heat of his laughing, honeyed eyes. "A bitty little elf drinking grown orcs under the table...we'd win every wager."

She laughed as he rolled to his back and quickly reclaimed her spot against him, pressing her cheek to the solid *tha-thump* of his heartbeat.

"I could be a full-time bar hustler," she smiled against his skin. "You could teach me how to hustle pool, too. I'd never need to worry about finding a better job or going back to school..." *Or finding a husband and trying for years to have a baby. I'd not have to worry about being good enough or pretty enough or charming enough, or spending my whole life in a pretty glass prison.* It was a wildly appealing thought, staying tucked away with him in this odd little town, living as close to a vagabond life as she could imagine. "...Nana would never be able to lecture me about getting married and carrying on the family legacy. Doesn't your family stress you out about stuff like that?"

It was an inappropriate question, nosy and far too personal, but

the boundaries of appropriateness were blurred with Tate; he was at once a polite gentleman and an absolute rake, had taken liberties with her from the moment he'd given her that cheeky wink at dinner, but she had allowed him to take them. Silva felt an unshakable certainty that despite her submissiveness, he would have backed off immediately if she'd indicated she wanted him to do so at any point in the previous two days.

"The only legacy in my family is to get a baby on some poor, naive lass and then promptly abandon them both." She winced at the flatness of his words, but Tate's hand stayed buried in her hair, lightly scratching her scalp. "Don't worry, dove, it won't be you. I'd need to double down on the heritage to keep up the tradition..." His eyes squinted in contemplation as he scratched his way down her neck. "Maybe a nice, sheltered cervitaur girl with harpy blood... if you happen to know one who wants to have her life ruined, send her my way." He tugged her hair lightly, and she felt her hackles rise at the thought. "Or rather, don't. I can't say it's a legacy I'm interested in continuing."

"Would...is that even possible? Don't harpies lay eggs?" Her nose wrinkled as she tried to remember if she'd ever known any cervitaurs. She considered the harpy who worked at the salon where she got her nails done; the woman had long, hooked talons and beautiful iridescent black feathers around her neck and shoulders, but Silva had never seen her standing. "Would a half-cervitaur still lay an egg if she has bird bits on the bottom?"

"Sweet Mab, I don't know...I hope not," he laughed as Silva twisted up to see his glinting smile.

"Have you ever *been* with a cervitaur? Do you think she'd still lay an egg? This place is really big, I'll bet you could fit an incubator if you took the pool table out." Her giggles were buried against his skin as he glared down at her.

"It was an off-the-cuff comment, and I regret making it," he sighed, as her shoulders shook with laughter. His talk of getting out of bed had stalled, and Silva pressed her cheek to his chest with a contented sigh, nosing his skin as his nails moved in soft circles over her back.

She wondered what his childhood had been like, if he'd gone to Elvish schools and lived in an Elvish community. Multi-species towns like Cambric Creek were far and few between, and even there she had gone to a private Elvish girls' school. It wouldn't have mattered in any case—Tate looked distinctly different from other orcs, but he was clearly Orcish. His lovely green skin and short tusks would have set him a world apart in the Elvish community, she knew without question. She didn't need to wonder what her grandmother would say if she brought an Orcish boyfriend home for Austalendë, even one of mixed blood. She was to get along with her neighbors and be a leader in the community, volunteer at the Ladies' Club, and be a gracious hostess at multi-species community events...but she was to marry an elf from a similar background as her, in the same social strata.

The right sort, as her grandmother would say. She was barely twenty-five, with another hundred and fifty years stretching before

her, and her entire life was planned for her already. *Freedom* was just a word in the common tongue dictionary.

"What's going to happen to me?" The words slipped out before she was able to control them; her internal anxieties bubbling to the surface and taking shape as a whisper against his smooth, pale green skin. For a long moment, he said nothing; only trailed a fingertip down her spine, making her shiver, before dragging it lightly back to her neck. When his fingers pushed back into her thick hair, Silva shuddered, leaning into his hand like a cat.

Her hope that he hadn't heard her was dashed when Tate began to speak in a low voice, his lilting accent giving false cheer to his words.

"You're going to go back to your life, little dove. You'll meet and marry some perfect, purple-skinned prat with a respectable, white-collar job and an excellent credit score. You'll kill yourself in the gym five days a week to keep this body because he'll let you know the minute you don't. You'll pop out a squalling brat to satisfy your family, and then get right back to the gym before it ruins your figure...It won't matter, because he'll already be fucking his secretary, or the nanny, maybe both, but he's like to do that regardless. By then you won't care, because you'll have your own pretty little doll of a daughter to fixate on, and you can pour all of your insecurities into her. You're going to do all the things proper little elves are expected to do."

Her eyes had gone wide as he spoke, goosebumps rising on her flesh once more, even though she was beneath the thick duvet. The air in her lungs had vanished, leaving her frozen and gasping, like a panicked fish, wheezing on a dock. She supposed his recitation of her future answered any questions she might have had about the depth of his Elvish background. Tate had perfectly described the lives of half the women at the club, at least two of her aunts, and most definitely her grandmother. The lump in her throat had the shape of her heart, and she struggled to swallow around it, left aching at the empty expanse of years that spread out before her, the prescribed script of her life.

She jumped when he spoke again, his hand skating down her spine once more.

"But then again, dove, the future isn't written in stone, and your life is your own to shape. You don't need to do any of those things, sweet Silva. And you'll have an escape that none of your perfect friends with their pretend perfect lives have."

He shifted her as he spoke until they were once more nose-to-nose on his pillow, flush to his warm skin. Silva felt the hard plane of him, leanly muscled arms and the smell of freedom encircling her. Her lips parted as his thumb lifted from the fluffy white sea of blankets to caress her chin, leaning in to feel the heat of his breath mingle with her own.

"I'll have you." Silva didn't know where the words had come from, nor why she uttered them, but they were a whisper of air against his lips, and Tate's mischief-filled, honey gold eyes danced.

"I'm not going anywhere," he shrugged gracefully. "You know where to find me, and you'll always have someplace to go...will you promise to come back and visit me, Silva of the nighttime?"

The rattle she felt in her bones at his innocently-spoken words, the frisson of electricity that shot through her veins when he kissed her—it was madness. She'd only just met him, after all, had fallen into his bed like an irresponsible student...but the thought of not seeing his laughing eyes and unsettling, too-wide smile again left her feeling hollow and empty, as empty as the thought of her predetermined life. She wasn't supposed to trust the fae, wasn't supposed to strike bargains or make promises, everyone with sense knew that, but his lips were still sweet as she whispered *yes* into his kiss.

She could always come back here, to his mischievous eyes and malevolent smile, to dagger teeth scraping her skin and the smell of freedom wrapping around her as she slept. Silva closed her eyes and pressed her face to his neck, breathing deeply, feeling as though the center of the heavy weight she carried with her every day had been cut away.

"You're so lovely, dove...so beautiful I could spend the rest of my days making love to you..." she shivered as his hand moved down her body in a sweeping caress, wondering if they were about to do exactly that. "...but if you think that means you can bewitch me into staying in bed with you all day, you're very much mistaken."

She let out an undignified squeak when the duvet was thrown back and whipped away, leaving her naked and exposed in the chill air, Tate's musical laughter echoing across the pressed tin tiles of the high ceiling. "Why can't someone else do it?" she whined, clinging to the pillow, lest he wrench that away as well.

"If you listen to my staff, it's because I'm an uptight control freak with trust issues...but I say it's my building, my rules. Now up you get."

Her eyes popped open at his words, just before he gripped her ankle and pulled her across the mattress as she squealed. She had thought he was a server, she realized, a bartender, albeit one who worked terribly long hours. The eclectic mix of old-world antiques and clean modern lines in this apartment matched the aesthetic of the bistro, where he'd seemed to have been every hour he hadn't been with her in the past two days. *You're so stupid.* She began to giggle as she rose from the bed, was nearly doubled over with her laughter when she joined him in the gleaming white shower and still tittered when his lips pressed to hers beneath the hot spray. It was only when he pressed into her that her manic laughter cut off on a high gasp that was nearly swallowed by the torrent of water gusting from the showerhead.

Her teeth were small and even and decidedly unsharp, but as she locked her legs around his slim waist, feeling the wet tiles at her back as he pumped into her, Silva dragged them over his skin, biting into his solid shoulder, trying to mark him as he'd marked her. There was nothing like his groan against her neck in her life at home, nor the way his hands tightened at her hips, hard enough to bruise her delicate lavender skin—only obligation and expectation and the suffocating sense that she'd never get to make a single decision for herself...but here she was free. As she convulsed around him, tightly gripping a handful of his long, wet hair, Silva wondered how long it would take until her resolve crumbled once she was home, sending her back to this place and his bed and his terrifying smile.

♥♥♥

The big bed was impossibly comfortable.

Lurielle stretched, feeling her back pop, and pushed her toes through the cool expanse of sheets until they met a solid mass, radiating heat. Khash's face was pressed to the pillow, facing her, and she took a moment to examine his sleeping form. Wisps of dark hair that had pulled out of his braid during the previous night now curled around his face, and the dark fan of his thick eyelashes lay upon his skin like a shadow. His tusks were massive, and his full lips were parted slightly as he breathed heavily into the pillowcase, sound asleep. She stretched forward until she was able to gently brush her lips to his, feeling her heart fold in on itself.

It was almost time to say goodbye.

She'd laid against his chest in a daze the previous night, while the rest of the fireworks display rained colored sparks over their heads. Her heart had been hammering as she recovered from her explosive climax, twinned in the thundering pulse beneath her cheek as he held her—a big hand splayed over her back, while the other gripped her thigh. Once the cacophonous grand finale reached its own climactic completion and the air grew still in the aftermath, Lurielle raised her head to gaze down at him. Khash's hooded chocolate eyes crinkled as he smiled his lazy smile at her, lifting his neck until he was able to meet her lips.

"Best fireworks ever."

She stayed there, resting against the steady beat of his heart as they talked in the darkness. She told him a bit about her relationship with Tev and how he'd treated her; the way she'd left, moving to

Cambric Creek for a job opportunity she wouldn't have pursued otherwise. She was the subject of hushed gossip in her mother's circles, she was sure, but she had long ago stopped caring, too happy with the life she'd built to miss anything from the life from which she'd walked away.

"Mmm, that man is fortunate he sleeps a long way away from me. You have a beautiful, brilliant elf in your life, and you don't cherish her each and every day? That's not a man, not where I'm from."

She'd snorted at the thought of Tev having cherished her even a single day, let alone doing so regularly. "What about you? I thought that was a song you knew all the words to?"

He hummed for a moment, dragging his palm down her back to squeeze the redolent flesh at her hip.

"Mhm, that I do. Five years. We met at a networking event, lived together for two of the five, but she didn't want anything more than that." His smile was swift, showing off the winking bands around his tusks. "At least, she didn't want it with me."

Lurielle harrumphed, not understanding how such a thing could be possible.

"Was she Orcish?"

"She was a half-orc, but she'd grown up in the city, not a part of any clan, We had about as much in common as you and I, at least in that regard. I grew up with a clan, so our experiences as orcs were mighty different. Not that different is bad, of course, but it was an obstacle. Tradition is important to me."

"Tell me more about it," she whispered, pressing her cheek to his chest, closing her eyes as his rich, deep voice painted a picture for her: one of great fires lit by his clan and the stories the elders would tell around them; fishing in creeks and playing in brush pine forests with his numerous cousins, the entire clan living in a closed community enclave. She could almost smell the sap of the pines, the hot southern sun baking the red clay hills in the high heat of the day, the smoke of the fires and the boom of other voices, all big and deep as the orcs gathered as a community around the flames. So wrapped up in his narrative, she was, that his next question caught her completely off guard, nearly startling her off his chest. "Do you not want kids then?"

She considered the question once she recovered, enjoying the feel of his thick fingers dragging over her shoulders, despite his guarded tone. "I do, I think...I just want them on my terms. No obsessive calorie counting and in utero painting classes and designer onesies. I'm not willing to give up my career and force my kids into moon dancing and basket weaving...yes, just on my own terms."

"Do I even want to know what in utero paintin' is?"

She lifted herself and grinned down. "You orcs think you're all so tough, but you have no idea. Elf culture is *intense*."

The walk back to his cabin was quiet, and she'd focused on the feeling of the balmy night air on her bare skin and the warmth of his hand in hers, and not the fact that she naked–outside, where anyone could see the least flattering bits of her.

The moonlight across his bed bathed her in a silvery-white beam when he kissed his way up her thick thighs, tusks scraping pleasantly against her skin, before delving his big tongue into her hot center. Lurielle tried to remember—as she gripped the sheets, her panting breaths seizing into strangled moans every time his full lips vibrated against her with the appreciative groans and grunts he was making—if her ex had ever gone down on her like a starved glutton at a feast, even once in their relationship. She was shaking with her climax against Khash's mouth before she was able to formulate an answer, her entire body seeming to pulse, glorious aftershocks rippling through her as he continued to lick her slowly until she stilled his movements with a hand to his head. Not even once, she'd decided. At least not like *that*.

"How's this going to work, darlin'?" he'd mused, climbing over her afterward, his huge body dwarfing her beneath him.

Lurielle watched the shadow of his erection bounce across the bedclothes as he moved, and couldn't hold in her laughter at the sight. "You're waggling," she'd giggled, pointing at the long outline before the shadow of her own hand closed around it. His big shoulders shook as caged her in his arms, insisting through his laughter that she was wrong, before silencing her with his lips.

Laughter in bed was another new sensation. Self-consciousness, awkwardness, mortifying embarrassment—all emotions she associated with intimacy, but laughter? She wondered what else she'd been missing out on. When his mouth latched onto the tip of her heavy breast, his thick, syrupy voice marveling over how *soft* she was, impossibly making it sound like a good thing, she had an idea it was more than just laughter.

Finding a position that was comfortable for them both took maneuvering, but when he'd pressed into her slowly, letting her adjust to his size as he groaned about how tight she felt, Lurielle felt a bright stab of clarity alongside the pleasure, seeing exactly how she'd wronged herself for years. She'd read articles in magazines and on blogs about women having the kinds of orgasms that made them see stars, go blind, nearly shake apart. Clickbait-y headlines and fictionalized accounts, she'd always thought, dismissing it as hokum, along with her Nana's warnings against wearing red on Mondays or instructions on how to honor the fae. Sex like that simply didn't happen in real life.

When she stiffened, unable to speak or blink her eyes, the only audible sound being Khash's voice in her ear as he pumped into her rhythmically, stimulating every inch of her with each deep thrust of his hips, she was forced to reconsider that she'd been wrong, wrong about everything she thought she knew, and probably owed Nana an apology.

"Who's wagglin' now, Bluebell?"

When he came shortly after, he lifted her hips, moving her body against him as he filled her with pulse after pulse of molten heat, Lurielle had been certain she could feel her soul leaving her body as she spasmed around him.

The moon had still been bright through the sheer curtains afterward,

Khash's big arm draped across her in the white light, as sleep pressed in on her. His head was pillowed on her breast, his exhalations heavy against her skin, and she had wondered if he would snore when on his back. *You leave tomorrow, so you'll never find out.* She knew her arm and leg were going to go numb under his heavy weight, that she'd need to shift herself into a new position before long, but sleep found her quickly, drifting away on the current of his warm breath against her.

Now, as light filtered in through the sheers, the sound of her phone, several rooms away, pulled her from her reverie. Squinting against the sunshine, she tiptoed through the cabin, retrieving her cellphone from her clutch in the bathroom. Several missed calls from Ris, and as many texts.

You should have come with me, I crossed everything off my bucket list!

Are you with Silva? Are you okay?

Lurielle if I don't hear from you in the next fifteen minutes I'm reporting you missing to the resort

It had only been a few minutes since Ris had texted last, she noted in relief, thumbing a quick reply. *I'm alive, you don't need to call out the hounds.*

ok, that's a relief

I didn't want to have to tell your mom where you were abducted

Lurielle snorted at the image of her mother's horror. She imagined her mother would decide to move away, possibly sequester herself, becoming a priestess on some remote island versus facing her friends at the club after news got out that her only daughter had been elf-napped in an orc nudist colony.

I can't wait to tell you everything on the way home

We have to be out of the room by 11, I'll put our bags in the car

She felt a slight pang of guilt, leaving Ris and Silva to pack up her things, but she'd made a point to keep everything relatively neat in her bag. She'd simply have to do the walk of shame in last night's dress...

Silva said she'll meet us for brunch at that same cute place, ok?

Let's shoot for noon

It was a few minutes before eleven, she noted. The walk from the resort to the little Main Street was less than fifteen minutes, and Khash's cabin another fifteen beyond that...she had at least another twenty-five minutes to stay snuggled at his side, she decided, setting the timer on her phone and tucking back under the blanket.

The minutes seemed to elapse in a handful of seconds. Lurielle felt an uncomfortable thickness in her throat, felt the rush of heat in her face that indicated tears would be forthcoming as she silenced the vibrating alarm. She stared at his face pressed to the pillow beside her—his strong jaw and dimpled chin, thick black hair and expressive eyebrows. He was charming and handsome and completely out of her league.

She'd never been terribly good at goodbyes. Khash barely stirred when she slipped from the bed, tiptoeing to the bathroom to shimmy into last night's dress. His breath seemed to stutter when she leaned back over the bed, pressing a soft kiss to his wide forehead, tears burning at the edges of her vision, but he remained asleep as she quietly pulled the door shut behind her with a click.

♥♥♥

Please tell me you didn't actually turn into a pumpkin

Her phone had buzzed shortly after the plate of food she didn't actually want was placed in front of her. Lurielle distracted herself with a bite of the orange blossom-infused crepes, closing her eyes to savor the delicate flavor, sipping her Bellini slowly. The sight of his name next to the notification on her phone's screen didn't surprise her, but she still felt her stomach flip all the same as she thumbed open the text.

I didn't

I had to meet my friends

checkout was this morning and the girls want to hit the road

There, she thought. Simple and straightforward, nothing to which he could take offense.

Why didn't you wake me up?

The question was accompanied by a frowning emoji with cross eyebrows, and she could clearly imagine his own thick, expressive brows turning down in the same fashion. Regret twisted her stomach as she pushed her plate away, feeling her face heat.

You looked very peaceful, I didn't want to disturb you

It wasn't a lie, she argued with herself. He *had* looked incredibly peaceful, sound asleep as he was, not even stirring as she'd kissed him goodbye...Lurielle bit her lip, turning her attention to the big window and the street beyond as tears threatened her vision. There were several clusters of patrons outside waiting for tables, and she immediately recognized the harpy and her gaggle of friends, all looking worse for wear from the previous evening.

The small restaurant had been crowded each time they'd been there, but that morning it was positively bursting with patrons. Sightseers, like them, toasting their debauched weekends before heading back to their lives, putting the events of the last forty-eight hours behind them. Here and there were tables for two: women of varying species sitting with orcs, playing at gallantry after having their fill of the nymphs and goblins and were-folk all weekend. She wondered if Khash would have taken her somewhere that morning, had she stayed; amusing her with his stories and charm before bidding her an awkward goodbye on the sidewalk. Best that she'd left it as is. *We're all just pieces of meat,* she reminded herself. *You don't need to feel guilty, none of this was real.*

Ris asked if there was anywhere else they wanted to go and Silva excused herself from the table with a squeak. Lurielle contemplated that she ought to join Silva, knowing herself well enough to say with certainty that the two Bellinis and glass of ice water would make themselves known approximately five minutes after they'd pulled out of town. Before she could remove the napkin from her lap, her phone buzzed again, as their fork-tongued server dropped the check on the table.

I wish you would have woken me up

♥♥♥

"Silva?"

She jumped when she realized she was being addressed and

pulled her eyes away from the flatware to look up at her friends. The spoon handles were fashioned into delicate silver branches, while the forks had a pretty flower and vine design. Mismatched but perfectly coordinated, particularly when they were paired with the pretty blue water goblets and embroidered table linens, placed there with her own two hands. She'd glanced up to the soaring ceilings in the bistro while she sat eating her breakfast at the bar, only to find familiar pressed tin tiles, answering her question about who was responsible for the interiors.

"Is there anywhere else you wanted to stop before we hit the road?" Ris repeated, gesturing to the line of small shops up the street.

"Oh! Um...no, I guess not...not unless there's somewhere else you wanted to go?"

Lurielle had been distracted since she'd arrived, picking at her food and staring blankly out the big window. She shook her head listlessly when Ris repeated the query and Silva felt her stomach flip, realizing it was time to leave. Excusing herself from the table, she wove her way through the busy restaurant on shaky legs.

It had been nice, seeing a different side of him that morning. They'd walked hand-in-hand up the block to the bistro, and she'd had fun helping set up the dining room, pushing a cart of the glassware from table to table, laying out the place settings as carefully as she did with Nana's fine china on Elvish feast days, while Tate scrutinized the cleanliness of the floors and restocked the bar. She'd examined the opening and closing checklists on the wall in the service hallway and

smiled at the tidiness of his small office—the tidiness of everything, she realized. She'd noticed how sparklingly clean the bathroom was that morning as they left the steaming shower, and every surface in the small restaurant was similarly spotless.

Silva snorted at the thought of Tate finding fault with the cleanliness of her imperious grandmother's stately home, wiping a long finger down the fireplace mantle or the legs of the dining room table with a disapproving scowl on his handsome face.

She'd stood beside him in the big kitchen as he made her french toast with vanilla crème fraîche and grilled peaches drizzled in honey, which she'd eaten perched at the end of the polished bar, sharing her plate with him as his employees slowly arrived. The staff—a motley group of pierced and tattooed tieflings and nymphs; a beautiful, willowy moth with pale pink skin and striking markings on her graceful, green wings, and several orcs—had regarded her curiously, but everyone had been friendly. When Elshona shouldered her way in, grumbling about her coffee already going cold, her dark eyebrows shot up at the sight of Silva, whose fork had frozen midway to her lips.

"Sleep well, lamby?"

The orc woman's smile had been sharp and knowing, and Silva felt her ears heat before straightening on her stool. "Very well, thank you. Not nearly long enough, though."

Now she stood in the pretty, clinically clean ladies' room, splashing cold water on her face in an effort to tamp back the tears that were threatening to form. The narrow hallway leading to the back-of-house was a bustle of activity, but Elshona smiled at the sight of her hovering outside the kitchen doorway.

"Heading out, lamby?" Silva stepped aside as Elshona barked orders in Orcish to the other two cooks in the kitchen before moving to the hallway. "We had a fun time, love, didn't we?" Her agreement ended on a gasp when the taller woman bent to lick at her ear, as she'd done the night before. "You're the most delicious little lamb chop I've ever had...don't let any of them langers back home give you a runaround, you hear? You're a star."

Her tattoos were covered by the long sleeves of her black chef's coat, but her eyes sparkled as she took the small elf in, still in her dress from the previous night. Silva was engulfed in the big woman's arms a moment later, squeezed tightly and given a kiss on each cheek, a whisper delivered to her temple.

"You watch yourself with him, lamb. His sort plays for keeps."

It was on the tip of her tongue to point out that she thought Tate and Elshona were the same sort, but Silva resisted, knowing her words weren't just about orcs and elves. *The right sort.*

The tiefling girl who'd been their server the previous morning had cornered her, along with the beautiful moth, questioning curiously if she was Tate's girlfriend, giving their opinion that they hoped so, because he *needed* a girlfriend, opining that maybe he wouldn't be so tightly wound if Silva was there to stay. Now the horned girl gave her a cheery smile and a wave as she moved through the dining room to deliver her last goodbye.

He was at the bar, filling champagne flutes that were whisked away by another server as she approached. Her throat was already thick when he looked up, giving her the same softer smile she'd been graced with the previous night when she'd hovered in his bedroom doorway. His teeth seemed shorter, less plentiful and sharp in the light of day, and Silva wondered if it was a trick of the light or a glamour he was able to control.

"No tears, dove."

She hadn't realized that the burn at her eyes had spilled over, not until he'd snaked an arm around her, pulling her to his hip before wiping away the moisture that tracked down her cheek.

"None of that. This isn't goodbye...not unless you want it to be."

She wondered if she'd be feeling the same way if she hadn't woken up at his side that morning, if she hadn't gotten a chance to see this different Tate: fussy and exacting, pinching the bridge of his nose as the moth and tiefling had cornered him over schedule changes they needed to make, the brisk control he seemed to have over the room. She knew that if she pressed her fingers into his loose bun, his thick hair would still be damp from the shower they'd shared; knew that the small crescent of her teeth was there on his shoulder, beneath his shirt, and that if she pressed her nose to the side of his neck he would smell like sandalwood and the wide-open sky.

She shook her head stubbornly.

"Well then...until the next time we meet, Silva of the nighttime."

His lips were soft against hers, an echo of the gentle kiss he'd pressed to her head the previous night in his bed, containing none of the animal heat and mischief of their other embraces. Silva wanted to lock her arms around his neck and refuse to let go, wanted to make more fae promises she knew she'd be forced to keep, but all that happened was him releasing her with a wink, the same with which he'd lured her in, before stepping away as his attention was pulled by a patron at the bar.

I'm glad you decided to come this weekend, Bluebell

Drive safely

Let me know when you get home

She exhaled sharply, staring out the window as rolling green hills and farmland passed by.

A heaviness sat in the car as they traveled home, and Lurielle wondered if they were all tinged with regrets over the way the weekend had played out. Ris kept her eyes fixed on the road, unusually quiet, not at all brimming with stories of her bonfire conquests or things she'd done. It was unlike her to not want to dish, and Lurielle wondered if her friend was feeling the ill effects of being treated like a piece of meat after all.

In the backseat, Silva was silent. Lurielle had been crossing through the dining room from the restroom when she'd happened upon the unexpected tableau of Silva and the handsome server drawing apart at the edge of the bar. He'd kept their bodies turned away from the open room, but in the reflection of the mercury glass at the bar's back, Lurielle had been able to see his hand leaving Silva's hip, as she stepped back with a stricken look. From the rearview mirror she could see that Silva's expression was blank, staring out her window.

For her part, she was unable to keep her thoughts off Khash. She wondered if she should have woken him up after all; wondered if they would have had that awkward parting, he might not still be keeping up the charade of acting the perfect gentleman. *Best to ignore him, block his number. Just put the whole weekend out of mind.* Good advice, solid advice, that she knew she ought to follow. She managed to listen to herself for a few miles more before thumbing open the phone.

I will

Have a good week

Her eyes burned at the memory of the fireworks, of his heartbeat, nearly in sync with hers underneath the wide, starlit sky.

I'm glad I came this weekend too

♥♥♥

PLAYORC
FOR YOUR PLEASURE !!
ORC SIZED!
02

Part 04

♥ *The Real World* ♥

The beef tip was bright red, faintly marbled with white and glistening. Lurielle watched in detached fascination as her boss lifted the absurdly small cocktail fork to his mouth, pointed teeth seizing the raw meat with a snap of his jaws. When he stirred the fork through the container, coating the next piece with blood from the bottom before lifting it to his lips, she shuddered.

It had been an endless week. Her team was being prepped on a new hydroponic contract the company had recently bid on, and there had been the typical posturing and in-fighting between several of the usual suspects on who would run lead, plus half a dozen meetings and conference calls, covering information which could have been easily communicated via

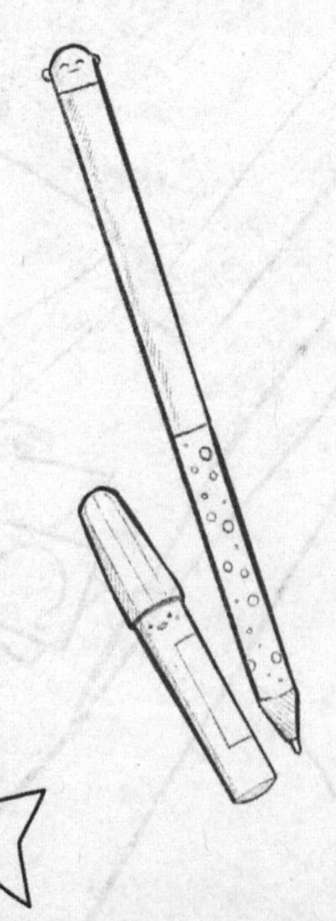

email. She had been glad for the distraction at first. Now though, several days back from their weekend trip, she was tired and cranky and more than ready for the weekend.

She was startled from her horrified observation of her boss's lunch by the unexpected buzz of her phone.

Happy humpday, Bluebell

This week has already lasted a hundred years

Why did we come back?

Lurielle stared at the screen, unable to blink for several long moments.

She'd cried out her sadness once her front door had closed behind her on Sunday night, and then again the night following—her regret over the way she'd left, her unshakeable certainty that she'd never meet someone as warm and funny as him in her everyday life, someone who made her feel beautiful and fearless—sobbed out on her sofa, under the spray of her shower, whimpered beneath the covers of her bed...and then she'd put her feelings away. It was a meaningless fling to which she'd assigned too much emotion, and she needed to let it go. Now she felt numb...and he was texting her.

Nearly an hour passed before she broke down and responded, unable to help herself once again.

It really has. Do you think we've fallen into some sort of time hole?

She wondered why she was indulging this, knowing it would hurt worse the longer she let things dangle.

I think you're right.

Was Lilypiddles very happy to see you Sunday night?

Lurielle felt all of the emotion she'd been tamping back rise up to the surface in a rush, and she leapt from the break room table, keeping her head down until the door to the ladies' room swung shut behind her. What was he doing? She was home, back to reality and work, sweating through aerobics and planting flowers in her yard on the weekend—there wasn't room for a make-believe relationship there. She wasn't interested in being someone he kept available for casual hookups, and she had no need for a text pal.

She enjoyed terrorizing my neighbor's cat all weekend

But she was very happy to sleep in her own bed

Lurielle bit her lip, hesitating as the stall next to her creaked open, the sound of the sink and hand dryer filling the tight space as she swallowed and typed.

Did Ordo enjoy being a hunting hound?

Khash had shared that he usually brought his big mastiff when he enjoyed pantsless time at his cabin, but that weekend Ordo had been pressed into service by one of Khash's brothers, who had wanted to take the big dog with him as he hunted in the mountains.

He did not

My brother said he was a big lazy baby

I reminded him that Ordo lives in a high-rise apartment and goes to a fancy groomer every month

She smiled, again imagining the big dog waiting on the doorstep while Khash trudged home with his split pants. She realized she'd not seen him undress and had no idea what kind of boxers he wore...her

musing was interrupted by another buzz of her phone

Can we have dinner this week?

Lurielle stared, not comprehending. The whir of the overhead fan was beginning to imitate something from a horror movie, setting her teeth on edge as her mind whirled. She had been a weekend fling, a piece of meat.

Tomorrow?

I can come to you

If you have plans already, maybe over the weekend?

She shook her head, attempting to clear her mind, in case she was hallucinating, but the text was still there when her eyes refocused. *What is he doing?!* Her heart was in her mouth, which explained why she suddenly felt it throbbing behind her eyes, in her ears, in her throat. The bathroom door opened again, the clipped voice of Silva's boss in the marketing department echoing off the tiles as she scolded one of her children on the phone. The walls of the room seemed to close in on her, the drone of the other woman's voice taking on an indistinct murmuration, and Lurielle gasped for air, suddenly feeling as though she were trapped in a great whirlpool, threatening to suck her down if she did not escape the bathroom's confines. Throwing open the stall door, she staggered to the sink, gripping the sides of the porcelain for an interminable moment before taking up her phone once more.

Tomorrow sounds great

♥♥♥

"How are we supposed to know how to start this thing? Do they think we're serving our own coffee at parties?"

Silva kept her smile firmly affixed, even though she was internally cringing at Lucidra's words. The elf at her back laughed her agreement, adding that "next they'll be expected to actually *bake* something for one of these events!" Her two companions laughed, and she stewed silently, her smile twitching. *They don't need to be such snobs...*

Silva leaned over the large coffee machine, shooing the other two volunteers away as she filled the water basin, expertly disassembling the stem and basket, as Tate had shown her the morning she'd spent with him in the empty restaurant. He'd stood closely behind her, a hand at her waist and his warm breath at her neck, instructing her step-by-step, before letting his teeth briefly graze her shoulder. She was nearly able to feel his warmth behind her now, flushing at the memory as she filled the machine on the fundraiser's dessert table, was able to feel his heat and his nearness...when a hand landed on her hip, she jumped, whirling around with a startled yip.

"Whoa! Careful now. You're quite the little expert, it seems."

He was the kind of elf she would have been starry-eyed over in undergrad—white-blond hair and high cheekbones, emerald green eyes and a tremendous air of confidence. She had completely forgotten about this fundraiser after the weekend, had thought of nothing but sharp teeth at her throat and honeyed eyes beside her, sharing a pillow. When her grandmother had called that morning, asking Silva what she was planning on wearing to the event that

evening, it had taken her several panicked moments to remember her commitment to the Ladies Club.

"I've done this before," she explained to the handsome elf, smiling demurely, confident that he wouldn't actually care enough to ask for details. She'd wondered, as she'd eaten the delicious breakfast Tate made for her at the little bistro's bar, how different Silmë elves were where he was from. She couldn't remember her father ever cooking for her and her mother, not even once, not even when she was very small. All Tate said, when she'd asked about his homeland, was that he'd emigrated from Ireland years earlier and had no intention of going back, giving her little clue as to the life he'd lived amongst the elves there. She wondered if this sort of elf—handsome and entitled, with the world at his feet—had existed in his world as well. *You'll meet and marry some perfect, purple-skinned prat.* Silva swallowed, suspecting she'd already been given the answer.

"Well, it looks like you ladies have been working hard...can I get you a glass of wine? I'm interested in hearing about your other volunteer work." Silva found herself being led across the big room by the handsome elf, abandoning her table, a glass of white wine pressed into her hand before she could think to protest.

Wynndevar was the kind of old Elvish name that hinted at an equally old, distinguished family, a family like hers, with deep roots in the community and deeper coffers. She learned he was from the larger city which bordered Cambric Creek and belonged to the club there; had grown up in the same world of cotillions and croquet and haughtiness that she had.

The right sort, she thought. It was almost as if her grandmother had created him in a lab.

By the end of the night he'd asked her out, and she'd gone home with dinner plans for the following evening and a twist in her guts.

Lurielle bit her lip, glancing every few seconds to the tab at the upper left corner of her screen. She'd opened the text app on her laptop nearly fifteen minutes ago but had still not sent anything. She would see him tomorrow, this time at a restaurant in the city, not far from his apartment. A real date, in the real world, with both of them on the same page. She scowled, moving the cursor to open the tab before she could overthink things any further.

The previous evening Khash had come to Cambric Creek as planned, plans made over the ladies' room sink and it had been a wonderful night until she'd almost gone and ruined everything. She'd watched in amusement as he polished off a second plate of pasta at dinner, in between asking her questions about the new hydroponic project she was starting. She should have realized, she'd thought, after witnessing him inhale an entire plate-sized steak for *dessert* that an orc-sized appetite was considerably larger than that of an elf. They'd walked down Cambric Creek's little Main Street afterward, her hand engulfed in his huge one. The sidewalk was evenly paved, but Lurielle had kept her gaze tightly trained to it, lest she look into the little shops and cafes around her adopted hometown, forever associating them with this moment. *When you wake up from this dream, you don't want real life to be ruined.*

"Do you have weekend plans? Could we maybe do something Saturday night?"

She'd looked up sharply, finding his hooded eyes trained on her, his full lips pulled into a soft smile, and her stomach flipped.

"What are we doing?"

He was so handsome it had made her breathless, especially in that moment, as he twinkled down at her. His eyes crinkled in the lamplight and her lungs tightened.

"Making dinner plans, I hope?"

She'd spent the entirety of the weekend at the resort wishing she had met him under different circumstances, that he was someone with whom she could walk down the street of her little town, that they could go on normal dates and bicker and fight and make up and be in love, like a real couple, in the real world. The fact that they were doing exactly that, less than twenty-four hours after she'd resolutely put her feelings away, reminding herself it was a meaningless fling in a place designed for hook-ups, had completely thrown her for a loop, and Lurielle felt as though she were straddling the line of both worlds, certain that she'd fall gracelessly into the center.

"No, I mean...what are we *doing*? I...I don't understand. I don't understand what you want, Khash, I don't understand what you're doing. This was a weekend fling! *Not* the real world. People don't have casual sex in nudist resorts and then start dating! I-I didn't think we'd see each other again, a-and I don't understand what you're doing." She'd watched as the smile dropped from his face, his wide brow furrowing. She hadn't liked the look in his eye and hated that she'd been the one to put it there.

He seemed to be speechless, for the first time in their brief acquaintance, no syrupy quip at the ready as his square jaw opened

and closed several times. She'd taken a step back as his arms opened in a giant shrug, holding them out like wings. "I...I'm sorry for wasting your time, then. It wasn't just casual sex for me. That's not what I want, Lurielle. That's not what I thought this was...but I'll respect whatever you want to do."

"That's *not* what I want," she'd cut in quickly, aware that they were probably a spectacle on the sidewalk. "That-that's not what I want at all. I just didn't think you...someone like you would ever be...I didn't know—"

"Aren't we both consenting adults, Lurielle?"

"Yes, but that's—"

"Don't *we* get to decide what the real world entails? What does that even mean, anyways? We met on vacation, don't people meet on vacation every day? If you don't want to tell our kids where we met, by all means, Bluebell, make somethin' up. But this *is* the real world for me."

Every breath in her body seemed to freeze, and the effort she'd been making to inflate her lungs had been abruptly cut off when he bent in half to meet her lips, his thick tusks gently scraping the side of her face, and the fight *whooshed* out of her as she gasped into his mouth.

When he pulled back, she'd felt dazed, the entire emotionally confusing week leaving her reeling. Khash was breathing hard through his nose, staring down at her...waiting, she'd realized. Waiting for her to make the next move.

The real world.

"Saturday sounds great."

Now she was annoyed all over again, and tapped out the text, hitting send before mortification could catch up with her lack of sense.

Look, there are some things you need to know if you want to date for real. My family is fucking crazy. I don't mean I have a zany uncle who wears a soup bowl on his head at Merryäle, I mean my mom is completely bananas, will hate that you're an orc, will probably bring a date for me the first time we have dinner with her and my dad.

She sat back, breathing hard. It was all true, and if he wanted life in the real world, he was going to need to deal with real world Bluebell. Leaning over the keyboard, she continued.

My panties are huge. They're high-waisted, they cover my whole ass. They're not sexy, they're not these tiny little things you'll want to take off with your teeth, but I'm not changing them for you. I'm not wearing thongs, I'm not wearing little hipsters. They're my underwear, I have to wear them, not you.

There was a brief lag as the message processed before a small green check appeared on the screen. *There. Let him be frightened away now,* she thought. Several minutes passed and she tried to refocus on her work, when her phone pinged, indicating a response.

Bold of you to assume that taking off giant panties with my teeth isn't my fetish

Her laugh came out as a strangled honk before she slapped her hand over her mouth, lowering her head in mortification when her co-worker glanced over curiously, as her notification pinged again.

I get a mani/pedi every month. I don't care if its not manly. I like the way it looks and I like having my feet rubbed. My granddaddy didn't come home every day from the mines with his hands caked in black for me to not have nice cuticles

This time her giggle was contained. Lurielle was perfectly able to hear his voice in her head, delivering his recitation of things his grandfather wanted for him. She *had* noticed, actually. His hands had been soft and smooth against her skin, with no ragged cuticles or hangnails. It fit his personality, she decided.

I hope you're good with a switch, because I'm gonna want you to spank me

She clapped her hand over her mouth once more, shaking in laughter. Somehow, that fit his personality as well.

I thought giant underwear was your fetish?

His response only took a few seconds and had her bouncing her in her seat with mirth and excitement, her ears flushed to a deep red.

I have a lot of kinks, Bluebell. Which you'll get to discover. But rest assured that big panties on beautiful girls with freckles and thick asses is at the top of my list.

I'm horny just thinking about it

The pompous voice of her team lead approached, and she knew it was time to focus. *You'll see him tomorrow night*. Her smile softened as she sent him a final message.

That's too bad because I need to get to work. We'll have to continue this later.

Lurielle bit her lip, feeling warmth in her chest that radiated to the tip of her nose.

I can't wait to see you tomorrow

Her message notification pinged a final time, just before she disconnected the app.

I'm counting the minutes, Bluebell

Have a good day

One date turned into two, and the days turned into weeks.

He was handsome and successful, she reminded herself daily, with a nine to five job and a standing racquetball match on Saturday mornings. Silva knew that he was a catch, knew that there were probably a dozen other elves lined up behind her, ready to take her place. The fact that electricity didn't thrum through her veins when he kissed her was simply a sign that she was free of fae trickery, she'd decided. The sex was adequate, they looked great together, and everyone around her seemed happy with their relationship. *This is what you're supposed to do*. Tate had left her with nothing more than a hazy maybe, not even his phone number, and the distance brought clarity—his nonchalance was surely a sign that he simply wasn't interested in hearing from her again.

There had been a moment of weakness, several weeks after returning to her life, several weeks into her new relationship, when she'd called the restaurant. She'd been invited to happy hour with Ris and Dynah, had indulged in too many of the fruity, potent house special, and had come home with an itchiness in her bones and a bravado that she didn't possess in the daytime.

She wanted to feel his teeth at her throat, wanted to be fucked in that big room with a cue ball in her grip, wanted to hear his lilting voice call her his dove, his Silva of the nighttime, and she *hated* him for it. She was *furious* with him as she stumbled into her moonlit apartment that night, enraged that he'd given her a taste of freedom, a glimpse of a life outside of the world she knew, only to set her free as if she really were the little bird he'd named her. Silva decided to call him, to call him out on the fact that she hadn't even warranted his number, her anger that he'd let her leave so casually, to rescind her affirmation that she'd see him again.

She realized she didn't know the name of the bistro when she attempted to search for it online. It only added to her anger as she stood at her sink, gripping her phone in her dark apartment. She could clearly envision the outside of the building: curling metalwork and sculpted boxwoods outside the doors, twinkling fairy lights strung across the small flagstone terrace...but no sign, no name above the door, nor on the building itself. She'd searched out the name of the hamlet, found listings for the resort, for the jewelry shop and the soap maker, the little store that sold locally made honey where she'd bought her jug of cider. Silva recognized the names of the other restaurants they'd passed, but there was no listing for Tate's bistro, and the map she'd pulled up on her GPS showed nothing on the corner where she absolutely knew it existed. In the end, she'd called the quiet restaurant across the street, where the girls had dinner the night she'd met Elshona.

"Clover. It's called Clover." The flat voice on the other end of the line had interrupted her stumbling question in an irritated tone before disconnecting abruptly.

Silva felt a shiver mover up her spine as she held the phone in her dark kitchen, typing in *Clover Bistro* into her search bar. The listing for the restaurant pulled up immediately, a small dot pinging on the map

in a spot that had been empty a moment before. *More fae trickery*, she sneered to herself contemptuously, recognizing as soon as she had the thought that it was likely just a clever marketing ploy. She'd punched in the number with fingers that shook with frustration and anticipation, recognizing the voice of the beautiful mothwoman instantly. Her own voice had come out like a croak when she asked for him, feeling her heartbeat behind her eyes, the confidence the fruity drinks had provided vanished in the moonlight of her empty kitchen.

"Where's Tate tonight?" she heard the moth ask someone else on the other end of the line. Silva's mind instantly conjured an image of him out with some lithe nymph, maybe engaged in an orgy with a buxom harpy and a graceful cervitaur, living his life completely free of obligation or expectation, nary a single thought of her in his head, not even letting his own business get in the way of his good time.

"Tate's tending bar at the Pixie all week...do you want to leave a message? He'll be here in the morning." She'd slid to the kitchen floor after turning down the offer of a message taken, her breath coming out in great shuddering heaves as reality cleared the cobwebs of her indignant imagination. He'd been at work all day, was still at work, no harpy or cervitaur there to distract him.

Unlike his bistro, the listing for The Plundered Pixie popped up immediately. Silva stared at her phone screen, able to perfectly envision the creaking sign and black painted bricks, the tall bar with the gruff-voiced orc and the little back room with the low sofas. If she called the little bar, she'd hear the ever-present amusement in his lilting accent, would imagine his cocky, crowded smile and laughing eyes and she would be lost.

The spot on her shoulder, where he'd bitten her, was still bruised, a deep purple flush marring her lavender skin. Silva wondered if she herself was the reason it had not vanished yet, for she'd developed a habit of pressing into it, her thumbnail approximating the sharp stab of his teeth. She'd pulled herself from the floor that night and stood under a scalding hot shower before bed, attempting to convince herself that her spiraling thoughts and frustrated tears were an unwelcome side effect of the fruity happy hour drinks she'd consumed and nothing more.

"I can't wait to meet this lil' killer."

Lurielle turned back to give him the stinkeye, her glare met by Khash's crinkled eyes and wide smile. "You just wait. Junie and I are a package deal, mister, so you'd better hope she likes you. She's never had to share me with anyone, so we'll see how you both do." He sobered instantly. Lurielle tried and failed to suppress her snort of laughter as the big orc gulped, his wide throat bobbing when the outraged Yorkie's head appeared at the window, her indignant yips meeting them as she slid her key into the lock.

"Hey now, none'a that, bunny rabbit..."

She watched, over the course of the following hour, as Khash got down on the ground, his big chin practically bumping the floor, working to win Junie over—playing with her squeaky ball, letting the little dog growl and nip as they played tug-of-war with her rope, and jump onto his chest to better bark in his face. Lurielle had merely needed to sit on the sofa in his apartment, letting Ordo lumber up and place his giant head in her lap for ear scritches, so she appreciated the extra lengths involved in winning over Junie. Khash was as tenacious and stubborn as the badly-behaved little dog, beaming triumphantly when the small bundle of fluff settled in the crook of his arm to sleep, and Lurielle climbed onto the sofa beside him to deliver a victory kiss.

Later—long after he'd placed Junie in her little bed with a blanket and stuffed elephant, long after she'd knelt on the shower floor to mouth at his straining cock, after he'd carried her to her bed and climbed atop her, holding her hips as he pumped into her slowly, after his eruption into her had necessitated the sheets being stripped, which he's helped her replace sheepishly—he held her against him, the tips of his fingers grazing the small of her back as she snuggled against his side sleepily.

"Who else do I need to win over, Bluebell?"

His voice was low rumble, sticky sweet honey, pulling her down. "No one," she mumbled into his skin. "Just Junie."

"Not your parents? Or your brother?"

Her brother lived on the other side of the country, and Lurielle only saw him a few times a year, while her mother could be notified of her new relationship in a few decades, she thought.

"Nope. I haven't even said anything to my parents yet. My mom will lose her mind when she finds out I'm dating an orc. I told you, she's one of those types."

"Is that what we're doing, Lurielle? Dating?"

He still had a way of saying her name like it was something exotic and sensual, his thick drawl coating each letter, pulling it like taffy. She raised her head to look up to his hooded eyes and lazy smile. "Do you have a better name for it?"

"Well," he began, pushing an unruly lock of hair behind her ear, "I told my parents my girlfriend is an elf...Mamma asked how serious we were, and I said very."

There was a flip in her stomach and a quiver in her spine at his slowly spoken words. *This was a meaningless fling a few weeks ago,* she reminded herself wonderingly. "That's a good answer. Let's go with that, okay?" His laughter was equally as slow, a lazy rumble against her as she resettled against his chest, a small smile tugging her lips as she drifted to sleep in his arms.

♥♥♥

The final heatwave of the year coincided with the start of the third month she'd been dating the handsome elf. He had charmed her family thoroughly, earning the firm handshake of her father and the cooing approval of her mother and grandmother both. Silva wondered if she would get a choice in the gilding of her cage, or if that decision would be made for her as well.

He'd suggested she ought to lighten her hair, the evening they'd gone to a concert in the park, after she'd mentioned her appointment the following morning.

"Something a little less...brown. You should definitely go lighter."

She'd felt her smile tighten at his words, although she'd said nothing. Her chestnut-colored hair was long and shiny and had never been tainted with chemical treatments before, and Silva wasn't inclined to start, regardless of how silvery platinum-haired he and his family were.

His apartment had been stifling as they returned from dinner that night, and Wynn had turned on the ceiling fan in the bedroom.

"If you turn down the thermostat we can snuggle under the blanket," she suggested with a smile, climbing onto the bed. "That's more fun."

He'd scowled from the bathroom doorway, pulling his shirt over his perfectly toned shoulders. "I don't want a blanket anywhere near me in this heat. Besides, it gets too cold with the air on." When her head found his shoulder beneath the thin sheet, once he had settled, she was dislodged roughly. "C'mon, Silva! Why are you so damned clingy?"

She retreated to the other side of the bed meekly, rubbing her jaw where his shoulder had clipped it, tasting blood on her tongue and tears burning her eyes, knowing she ought not to cry, as it wasn't the first time that he'd been less than gentle with her. The spot on her shoulder seemed to pulse as she pressed it beneath the sheet, wishing she was in a different bed, wishing she could feel the security of strong arms wrapped around her as she slept, wrapped in a cocoon of freedom.

♥♥♥

She winced as he rolled through the mud, several other orcs piling on top of him. It was the third week she'd come to watch him play in his Grumsh'vargh league, sitting on the end of a long bench with Ordo lying at her feet. This week, the cluster of orc women who had been there every other time she'd attended had been sitting closer than normal to where she shifted, alone on the bench.

"Sweetie, what in the world is a tiny thing like you doing here? Dog walking?"

The big mastiff flicked his ear back as though he'd heard himself referred to. Lurielle smiled down at him, giving him a scratch. A gentle giant, Ordo had proven to be easily cowed by Junie's bossy yipping, allowing the little Yorkie to sit on his back whenever they were together.

Lurielle took a moment to breathe, fixing her face. It wasn't the first time they'd encountered comments and looks for being in an inter-species couple, she reminded herself, and it certainly wouldn't be the last. "I'm here to watch the match, actually." She kept her voice even and her smile serene, her gaze trained on Khash as his squad reformed for the last play of the game. He was covered in mud, and dried blood formed a crusted line from his nose to his dimpled chin, but Lurielle did love the way his round ass and thick thighs filled out the white uniform shorts. When she straddled his hips later, rolling herself against his thick length as his mouth clung to the pebbled tip of her breast, she was reminded that it didn't matter what anyone else thought or said. They were happy, and that was all that mattered.

"Tell me again what the point of this is?" Ris eyed the clusters of tables around the room. She'd thought speed dating had died out in the previous decade, but the crowded coffee shop said otherwise. Beside her, Dynah huffed, pulling out her phone as the notification for the dating app chimed.

"The point is to meet someone! C'mon, don't be so cranky, we came all the way to the city to widen the pool. I told you that you shouldn't have deleted the app, I'm blowing up over here!"

She had indeed deleted the app, after the string of disastrous dates she'd endured in the past several months. One after another, each as unsatisfying as the next, the men she met through Dynah's dating app were either ridiculously entitled, thoroughly uninteresting, or clearly only after one thing. A gnoll who answered calls from his mother several times during their dinner date, a tiefling with whom she'd had not a single thing in common, a human who was obviously only interested in being able to say he'd slept with an elf.

The night she'd agreed to meet a middle-aged werebear for drinks had been the tipping point. She'd been surprised when they'd matched—he was a bit older than what she normally went for, but his profile had been interesting, his photo distinguished, and he'd messaged her first. *Why the hell not? He's got to be more mature than the mamma's boy, right?* It had been an old picture, she'd seen at once, entering the trendy tequila bar that night. His photo had shown salt-and-pepper hair and smiling eyes in a lightly lined face; a face that had been pinched in a sour look as she approached. His salt-and-pepper hair had lost all of its pepper since matching with her, she thought ruefully, and his face was creased with more years than his profile had advertised.

She took note of the way his expression brightened for the pretty server, a doe-eyed goblin who appeared to be around Silva's age, if not younger. When he had the temerity to question *her* age, insinuating she looked older than what she'd listed on her profile, Ris remembered there was a book waiting for her at home and that she liked herself far too much to put up with such an asshole.

"Well, this is actually what women in their thirties look like," she'd laughed, draining her glass before retrieving her purse from the back of her chair. Tossing a twenty on the table, she'd left him sputtering, turning to the door without guilt. There had been a familiar face at the bar as she passed, a cocky minotaur with whom she dallied before, always up for a good time. Unlike her date, he was friendly and charming, and she'd not spared a look back to the werebear when he'd left with her.

"Did you make the reservations yet? Just let me know how much I owe you...I can't wait! An orc buffet is exactly what I need to forget all about Grovan."

Ris pursed her lips at Dynah's words, sighing. She'd not planned on returning to the nudist resort, had experienced it once and had

her trove of only slightly embellished stories to tell from the weekend spent there, and had no reason for a repeat performance...but it would be easy, she thought. Easier than this, at the very least. "I'll make them online as soon as I get home. Let's get out of here, okay? This is going to be an exercise in frustration, I can already tell."

She wondered, as they stepped into a wine bar down the street a few minutes later, if the second trip would yield the same results. *There's only one way you're going to find out...*

♥♥♥

They'd been out for dinner with her parents when her mother had insisted she and Wynn pose for a photo in front of the shallow falls that ran through Cambric Creek's small downtown. He'd scooped her up and they'd smiled brilliantly for the picture, but then he'd staggered comically, holding his back and loudly proclaiming that she ought to start laying off the desserts when he'd set her back on the ground. He and her parents had a good chuckle, but Silva just glared. *You'll kill yourself in the gym five days a week to keep this body, because he'll let you know the minute you don't.*

The weeks passed. It was lonely on her side of the bed at night; his apartment in the city felt cold and unfamiliar, and she was sick of it. She was sick of it, and she didn't need to put up with it. *You'll always have someplace to go...* His skin was warm when she slid to the center of the mattress, pressing her cheek to his side. He did not turn, his arms never coming around her, and she felt her resolve grow, along with her anger.

"Silva..." Wynn's voice was irritated, and she glared at his back.

"Why won't you cuddle with me?" she demanded. "I'm not asking you to not sleep, but why can't you sleep *with* me?" His annoyed response could barely be heard over the blood rushing in her ears. She was certain his behavior could be classified as a runaround, could practically hear Elshona's blunt advice. She didn't need to wonder what Wynn's answer would be if she asked *him* to get up and make her old country comfort food at this time of night.

Her dress was on the bench at the foot of the bed, and her hands found it in the darkness of the room—pitch-black, even though she'd expressed her desire to have one of the shades partially up, as she didn't like the impenetrable darkness—as she stumbled to the dimly lit bathroom to pull it over her head.

"What are you doing?" Wynn snapped as she crossed the room. She'd already thumbed open the rideshare app, knowing that cars in the city were in fast supply; there would be one waiting for her at the curb seconds after she tapped the screen, which she did then.

"You want to sleep alone, Wynn," Silva said in a flat tone that she almost didn't recognize as being her own. She wasn't going to be her grandmother, wasn't going to be her aunt. Her life was hers to shape. "So I'm letting you."

The car was waiting at the curb, as she'd known it would be, whisking her back to Cambric Creek and her own bed, where she'd be happy to sleep alone for the foreseeable future.

She had tried, Silva reminded herself, as she ran a brush through her shiny hair the following morning, as she fastened her earrings before work. She reminded herself as she smiled her bright smile, greeting the security guard at the office door and chatting cheerfully with her co-workers, before settling at her cubicle with grim determination. She had tried, and no one could say otherwise.

It had been three months since she'd taken that weekend trip with Lurielle and Ris, three months of throwing herself back into the dating scene and volunteering and everything that she was supposed to do, all the things that made her *the right sort*. She'd tried. Every step she took that morning had a click of a surety she hadn't felt in ages, for she had tried and she was done trying.

Lurielle was leaning on the counter in the otherwise empty break room when she came in to top off the hot water for her tea. Ris and Dynah had filled her in on the gossip she'd been oblivious to since she'd been dating Wynn—Lurielle was seeing someone, no one had met him yet, but she seemed completely over the moon.

"I am absolutely *not* going naked horseback riding, so you can just stop suggesting it!" she'd been exclaiming with a laugh as Silva entered the room, ears darkening when she saw she was no longer alone before turning towards the refrigerator. "What time are you leaving today? Please make you bring his good leash–oh! Don't forget his stuffed duckie! It's his favorite...ok, Junie and I will see you in the morning, drive safe."

Silva smiled into her paper cup as Lurielle's ears darkened further, mumbling something Silva couldn't quite catch before disconnecting the call.

"Fun weekend plans?" she asked with a smile once Lurielle turned back around, pulling a sleeve from the dispenser of the coffee machine.

"We're going away for the weekend and he always manages to forget something!"

Silva seated herself at one of the round tables, sipping her tea. She was going to call Wynn when she got back to her desk,

she told herself, call him and end it. She had tried, and her future wasn't set in stone.

"How have you been?" Lurielle asked, pulling out her own chair. "I feel like I've been non-stop since we started this hydroponic thing... Dynah said you're seeing someone?"

It was her turn to flush, nodding slowly. "Since the week we got back from our trip but...but I'm breaking things off with him. Today, actually." She was surprised when her awkward laugh had the wobble of tears. "He's not very nice to me." Silva felt a shudder run up her back as a hand closed over hers, where it rested next to her paper cup of tea.

"Then that's for the best, Silva," Lurielle murmured evenly with a furrowed brow. "You deserve someone who *is* nice to you, and that's a pretty low bar, to be honest. You're super sweet, you're smart, you're beautiful, everyone loves you...any guy would be lucky to have someone like you as a partner, and if this guy doesn't recognize that, then his loss."

She nodded, knowing Lurielle was right. She had tried. "How did you do it?" she blurted out, feeling heat steal up her neck. "H-how did just...stop caring? I mean...how did you walk away?" Pressure built in her face, and Silva considered that she'd cried more in the past three months than she had in the entire year. "I-I don't feel like I'm ever going to be allowed to make a single decision for myself."

Lurielle sat back in her chair, considering the younger elf before shrugging. "I just...did, I guess. It was a long time coming though.

I'd had enough of feeling like I wasn't good enough, never feeling comfortable in my own skin."

Silva nodded as Lurielle hesitated, gripping her cup tightly before continuing with another shrug.

"Nothing I did was good enough for my mom. She drove me crazy about finding a boyfriend. I started dating Tev, then it was 'why aren't you engaged yet?' She didn't like the clothes I wore, would constantly drag me shopping and force me into clothes that didn't fit my body type, *then* be mad that nothing looked good on me."

Silva peered over the rim of her cup as Lurielle took a gulp of her coffee. She'd flushed as she spoke, the tips of her long ears a dull pink, but plowed on once she'd swallowed.

"They always made me feel bad about my body, her and Tev both. I expected it from her, but from him it was like...why are you with me then? I felt bad about myself so I didn't want to go out, didn't want to go anywhere, which just made it worse. Tev wasn't nice to me either, so please take it from someone older who's been there, Silva...you don't need to put up with that. There are good guys out there, don't settle. Don't let someone else make the decision of what's right for you."

The future isn't written in stone.

"Your new boyfriend's not like that?"

Lurielle's eyes softened at the question, a smile pulling involuntarily at her full lips, and Silva felt a tug of envy for the immediate change in her friend's demeanor.

"No, he's...he's not like that at all. He makes me *feel* beautiful. He says it too, and that's nice, but he makes me feel it, which is just...I've never had that before. He's amazing, total package, but Khash acts like *I'm* the catch!"

"But you *are* a catch! And you're brave! I-I wish I could be that brave."

Silva of the daylight hours was a meek, obedient little mouse, after all. *Your life is your own to shape, dove.* Tate's voice was a distant curl around her ear, and the bruise on her shoulder tingled.

"You *can* be," Lurielle countered, leveling Silva with a serious look. "You can be, Silva. Your nana isn't going to be around forever...do you really want to be stuck for the rest of your life with the choices you made just to make her happy for a few years?"

Two other employees entered the room then, and the conversation lapsed. To her relief, Lurielle didn't use the interruption as an excuse to leave. "So," Silva murmured, clearing her throat once the room was empty once more, "naked horseback riding?"

Lurielle squeaked, hiding her face as her shoulder shook in mortified laughter. "My boyfriend thinks he can sweet talk me into anything," she laughed, "but I am *not* doing that!"

"What kind of stable even offers such a thing?!"

Lurielle gave a swift glance around the room, ensuring they were still alone. "The place we went on our trip. That's where we met."

Silva felt her jaw drop in shock. The night she'd met Elshona, the night Lurielle had looked so pretty, not going with Ris to the bonfire party...the ramifications hit her with the force of a freight train. "Your boyfriend is an *orc*?!" she gasped. "Did-did you tell your mom?"

"Not yet," Lurielle admitted. "She's going to lose her mind, which believe me, is another check in his favor." Silva dissolved into giggles as Lurielle continued. "We're going back up to the resort this weekend, just to relax, we've both been going non-stop with work."

Silva recovered from her mirth, sobering instantly. Back to the resort, to the little town, where Tate was. *You can't tag along, they don't want you as a third wheel.* "Oh," she said in a small voice, feeling her heart thump in her chest, the bruise on her shoulder pulsing in response, "and you're leaving tonight?"

"Well, Khash is leaving this afternoon, he's only working this morning. I'm not going to get out of here until this evening, so he's going up with his dog today to open up the cabin. He lives in the city, so it's not like we'd be going home together anyways. I'm going to leave early tomorrow morning."

"Could-could I go with you?" Silva bit her lip as soon as the blurted request left her lips. "I mean...I don't want to put you on the spot, and I don't need to be entertained or anything, I-I have someplace to stay. It's just..." It would be a built-in excuse to go, if her family questioned where she was for the weekend; she was taking a girls weekend with her friend, and she wouldn't be around to field Wynn's calls, if he bothered. She'd see Tate and his laughing eyes and dagger-toothed smile; would fulfill her promise and get to feel the security of his arms. *Freedom*...

"If you have a place to stay, I'd be happy for the company," Lurielle smiled, glancing up as several people shuffled into the room, lining up at the coffee machine. "But I'm going to want to hear everything on the drive."

There was a spring in her step as she marched back to her desk. A department email to forward, several files from her boss she needed to parse through, several clients to contact...but her cellphone was there, an inescapable presence on the edge of her desk, calling to her from its ice cream-colored case. Scooping it up, Silva flipped open her contacts before she could overthink her actions.

"I don't think we should see each other anymore," she said calmly, in a voice that was not her own, with bravery she must have leached from Lurielle during their talk. "You don't seem happy with me," Wynn's voice sputtered denial, but she continued steadily, "and I'm not happy with the way things have been going. I think it'd be best if we end this now." When his sputtering turned to anger, Silva disconnected the call, blocking his number. Another layer of the heavy weight sliced away, leaving her with a giddiness that made her bounce in her chair. The rush of adrenaline she felt directed her movements before she could stop herself, and then she was thumbing open her contacts once more, swiping until she reached the number she'd saved for Clover Bistro. She'd leave a message with the beautiful mothwoman today, she decided, would let him know she was coming.

The moth did not answer the phone. Instead, Tate's lilting accent froze her in her chair, completely unprepared. Still jocular, she was able to envision his cocky smile and messy bun, leaning behind the polished bar, or perhaps in his tidy office. Amusement colored his voice as he repeated his greeting, and Silva jolted, realizing she'd remained silent, unable to force her throat into action.

"Dove, is that you?"

♥♥♥

The dining room was a bustle of activity.

Silva beamed as she took in full tables, the gleaming dark-wood bar, the familiar sight of the pretty glassware, and pierced staff. The beautiful mothwoman was at the hostess stand, a small queue in front of her, and she saw several servers she recognized moving between tables.

Tate was nowhere to be found. She suffered a momentary flutter of self-consciousness that he wasn't there and that she wasn't welcome after all, but shook her head firmly, clearing the doubt away. If he wasn't here, she would go to the bar, would read a book at the restaurant across the street until he made his presence known; she would spend the weekend in his arms and demand something more from him before she left Sunday, something more tangible and significant than *til the next time*. A promise, she thought. She'd extract a promise from his lips, one that he'd be bound to keep.

She sensed him behind her before she could even turn around. The tiny hairs on the back of her neck rose, and Silva shivered, feeling as though she was being stalked; a pard with great jaws, creeping on her steadily, heat at her back and a whisper of sandalwood in her nose. The noise in the dining room was suddenly a distant, white noise, and she wondered, as she allowed herself to be easy prey, if this moment existed in some liminal space, between what was and what would follow, in the faerie realm.

"You look lost, little dove."

Silva stood stock-still as he raised a long-fingered hand, dragging lightly up her arm to her neck. Tate pushed the heavy curtain of her hair over one shoulder, exposing her neck, the spot where he'd bitten her just out of sight, beneath her silk shell. A shiver moved up her spine as he bent his head to move his nose up her neck, breathing her in, ending in a soft kiss behind her ear.

The room hummed in a blur, and Silva was certain they were invisible where they stood, on the dining room floor.

His hands dropped to land on her hips as she turned in the circle of his arms. His almond-shaped eyes were lit with mischief, honey gold and dancing as he took her in, his mouth pulled into its ever-present cocky smirk.

"Not lost," she corrected with a smile, gratified when his mouth split and his smile stretched, revealing the long spikes of his teeth, longer than she remembered, but perhaps that was only here, in this non-space where they stood. Sharp and crowded, she wanted to feel their drag upon her skin. Silva rested her hands against his leanly-muscled chest, a gesture of pushing him away...until she fisted her fingers in his shirt, preventing him from escaping her, and his smile widened impossibly further. Lovely green skin and Elvish manners, but more fae by far.

"I'm exactly where I meant to be."

The sunset was a crimson smear at the tree line at the crest of the hilltop, bathing the valley below in pink shadows, thin tendrils of golden light barely touching the rich green vegetation. Lurielle stretched and sighed, rubbing her face to the broad forest-colored chest beneath her cheek, completely at peace.

When he'd announced he was putting up a hammock, she'd thought he was kidding.

"Darlin', my granddaddy wants me to have a hammock, you don't understand. 'You work hard, boy, you deserve to put your feet up at the end of the day!' He's telling me right now!"

"I don't disagree," she laughed, "but isn't that what your butt massager chair is for?"

The first time she'd been to his apartment, she'd been introduced to the giant leather club-style chair. Sleek and expensive-looking, the mahogany leather was accented with a brass nail head trim, and a full control panel on the inside of the arm. Heat, vibrations, a reclining back and rolling knobs that massaged her shoulders and, as she learned with a squeak, lower half.

He'd regarded her with a frown. "I can't take my chair to the cabin, Bluebell."

Her boyfriend was, she'd learned, far from perfect. His winsome smile and Old South persona meant she was often left cooling her heels, tapping her fingers impatiently as he worked to charm virtually every server, mail clerk, usher, and sanitation worker they came across on a weekly basis. He drove too fast, snored like a foghorn. Stubborn as a bull, she questioned whether he had minotaur blood often, for once he latched onto something, there was nothing she or anyone else could say that wouldn't make him dig his heels in.

The hammock was orc-sized and had taken several trial-and-errors, resulting in her hiding her giggles as he picked himself off the ground, cursing in Orcish and kicking the giant ball of netting, to determine the proper tension required to secure it between two great trees. Climbing into it was still terrifying, as was rocking out of it, but Lurielle had to admit, as they swayed in the golden sunset, it was one of his better flights of fancy.

"Granddaddy did a good job picking this one out," she murmured across his chest, smiling against his skin when his rich chuckle rumbled beneath her cheek. *Pantless Time with Bluebell* had become something she'd become gradually more comfortable with, as long as they weren't doing anything more taxing than laying in the hammock or swimming in the lake.

She was concerned about Silva, even more since telling Khash that she'd dropped her co-worker off that morning in town. "She said she has someplace to stay," she'd shrugged, when he'd questioned the whereabouts of her travel companion. "I think she fooled around with a server at that cute little bistro on the corner of Main Street the last time we were here, I'm pretty sure that's who she's staying with. He's cute, but...I don't know, there's something a little creepy about him. He has too many teeth."

Khash had whirled around from where he was measuring dog

food into bowls, earning an annoyed bark from Junie for his slowness. "Is he an orc?"

"Yes. He's a lot shorter than you, though, and thinner. Probably because he doesn't eat thirty-two ounce steaks for dessert."

Khash's brow was furrowed, grunting as he lowered the two bowls to the ground for the waiting dogs. "His name is Tate, and he's not a server. He's the owner, owns the bistro and the bar and a patch of the sidewalk, and spirits save you if you fuck with his sidewalk, he will rain fire and damnation upon you. The village council wanted to repave everything a few years back, take out the old bricks and the cobbles and he brought in lawyers to stop them from touching the corner, said it would 'ruin his aesthetic.' He's a real nasty piece of work, I've heard, I would *not* trifle with him...he's fae, you can't trust any of 'em. How did she get mixed up with him?!"

Lurielle shrugged, frowning. "I'm honestly not sure, but it's Silva. At most she let him kiss her hand as they crossed the street. I told her we'd meet her for lunch on Sunday before we leave so you can meet her, are you going to have a problem going there?"

Khash scoffed, topping off the dog's water bowl. "Not at all, it's the best restaurant downtown, no question. Always a wait for a table. I said not to trust him, not 'don't eat his food.'"

Now she pushed thoughts of Silva out of her mind as twilight settled over the hills, enveloping the little cabin in shadows, Khash's thick finger dragging around the curve of her breast. Soon it would be too cold for pantless time, he'd lamented earlier, but Lurielle was looking forward to weekends in the snow, curled up in front of a big fire against his side.

The first strike sounded low, and she tilted her chin up just in time to see the first burst of sparks overhead. She needed to tell her mother, needed to tell her family that she'd met someone, was in love, regardless of what they would say or think.

"Bluebell, they're playin' our song," he murmured into her hair as the fireworks boomed through the valley.

Beside the hammock, Ordo whined in distress, deep in his throat. Junie barked in response, from her customary perch atop the big mastiff's back, and Khash clicked his tongue.

"C'mon now, don't let that little ball of fluff show you up. Nothin' to be afraid of."

The big dog dropped his head in defeat as Junie yipped in triumph from his shoulders.

"Look at the two of them," Lurielle giggled. "Like a little flower and her bunny rabbit."

It was her fault, he would say later. Her fault for the way she laid against him, for unevenly distributing their weight in the mesh; her fault for making him sit up, pushing down on the side of the mesh and upending them in a pantsless heap on the ground. She clung to him, giggling in the grass as color exploded overhead. She loved him, and she didn't care what anyone thought, or how preposterous it was that she'd found love on a weekend trip to a nudist resort.

"You are gonna pay for that, Bluebell," he growled, staggering to his feet. His huge outline blotted out the hills, haloing him in color, his enormous cock swinging before her.

"You're waggling," she giggled, unable to help herself. She let out an undignified shriek when he hauled her up, throwing her over his shoulder and gripping a handful of her not-at-all toned ass.

"We'll see who's wagglin', Bluebell."

The fireworks had reached their zenith, the grand finale exploding overhead as Khash carried her back to the cabin. Color and explosions, she thought, in between her hysterical laughter.

Playing their song.

♥♥♥

The Girls will return in ***Parties***, coming Summer of 2021

Read on for a hint of what's to come!

♥♥♥

The ballroom was draped in pink. Pink chiffon swags, pink table linens, pink uplighting. Enormous vases of pink and white flowers graced each table, and the birthday girl herself was dolled up like a poofy pink cupcake. Lurielle loved her grandmother dearly and was thrilled that they were able to celebrate her two hundred and fiftieth birthday at all, but Nana's choice in decor was reminiscent of something a princess-obsessed preschooler might have chosen.

She watched in amusement as one of the waist-coated servers made a wide arc around the table where she sat with her boyfriend, the tray of hors d'oeuvres he carried completely unmolested by disinterested elves. Beside her, Khash grunted in frustration.

"Now you know he's doin' that on purpose," he grumbled, balling up his pink cloth napkin in frustration, as Lurielle snorted into her drink.

She had tried to warn him.

"I thought I asked you to order food while I showered?"

Khash had scowled at her in the mirror as he expertly twisted the long ends of his silk tie into a large Windsor knot, earlier that same evening. "Bluebell, you know we don't have time for that, we need to get ready. You mean to tell me there's not going to be food there? At a dinner reception?" He'd rolled his eyes at her reflection as he pulled

on his suit jacket, an endless expanse of expensive grey wool, and fussed with his contrasting pocket square.

Lurielle just glared. *Fine. If he wanted to be a know-it-all, let him find out the hard way.*

She had yet to determine if all orcs ate as much as Khash did. She'd tried to pay attention when they went out together, would look for other orcs in restaurants, trying to determine if they too had ordered two entrees and an appetizer at dinner. She'd once stalked an orc around the grocery store, surreptitiously peeking into his cart to scan the contents, and had once espied Silva's slender Orcish boyfriend through the wide window of his small restaurant one weekend afternoon, sitting in front of a laptop at the end of the bar, eating an apple. Lurielle hadn't noticed a steak dinner hidden beneath his screen, as she'd pointed out to Khash later. His nonchalant rebuttal had been that the other orcs in restaurants were on dates and were clearly holding back as they attempted to woo their intendeds and that Silva's fae boyfriend didn't count.

Khash had harrumphed when they first entered the cotton candy-hued hall, seeing the fusty servers gliding around the room, bearing trays laden with bite-sized delicacies. He'd glanced down with furrow between his full brows when she hadn't responded with an elbow on her hip and a derisive snort of her own, the anticipated reaction to such a scene. Khash never expected her to be anything but what she was, and the freedom to be a smartass on main, the ability to be her uncensored self was intoxicating, but she didn't dare display anything other than a beatific smile, keeping all traces of opinions or disagreeableness or personality, anything that might warrant the negative attention of her mother, deeply buried.

Being there as herself—short, slightly overweight, unmarried and childless—was enough of a crime. Adding an Orcish boyfriend to the list of offenses was practically unforgivable.

She hated events like this.

She'd always been the outcast among her elegant, glamorous relatives—short when they were tall, soft and round where they were concave and willowy. She'd always been more interested in hiding behind a book than in flirting with the handsome elves at the country club, and now she was surrounded by all of them—distant relatives she saw rarely, plus the ones she'd grown up with, all crowding around with knowing smirks and curious glances. Lurielle was sure it was common knowledge throughout the extended family that she'd had a huge falling-out with her controlling mother several years earlier, that she'd left her fiancé and moved away, far from the constrictions and expectations of Elvish culture and society.

Now here she was: stuffed into a body shaper that displaced her internal organs with her huge, orcish boyfriend, attempting to keep her smile from appearing to be a grimace. She had nothing in common with the people who shared her blood, and likely never would. She hated events like this, but having him here, despite increasing the amount of attention she might have received otherwise, was a security she'd not trade for the world.

"Oh, I can guarantee he's doing it on purpose," she agreed as the server disappeared into the swinging kitchen doors with his still-full tray, draining her glass before stretching up to kiss her boyfriend's broad cheek.

♥♥♥

She'd wound up at the little black-bricked bar that night as a change of pace from the previous evening. Silva was the one who had mentioned it, when Dynah asked their straight-laced co-worker what she'd done in lieu of the more carnal activities the little town boasted. Silva had blushed prettily, mumbling about there being a nice little bar where'd she'd gone, where everyone kept their clothes on.

The orc who watched her now did indeed have his clothes on, although Ris had the distinct impression he was envisioning her without the same modesty. He was not her normal type, she thought, covertly looking him over, deciding that he seemed vaguely familiar to her. He was slimmer than the others of his kind from the pool the previous night—great, hulking brutes with deliciously muscled arms and straining cocks, eager for her to stoke them and suck them, to push her to her knees and spread her legs, taking their pleasure before moving on to the next mouth. She'd had better luck at the tiki bar pool now that the season was winding down, compared to when she'd been here with Lurielle and Silva. It was very nearly too cold to go around naked, and the throngs of other *sightseers* who'd clogged up the decks and restaurants the last trip were mostly absent now.

Despite having better "luck" this time around, she'd left the pool the night before more than a little aggravated with the lack of reciprocity she'd found from the crowd of orcs. The guys there that night were all horny and eager to get off...but they'd evidently been spoiled by the plethora of easy sex all summer, and expended very little effort in return. Reminding herself of Silva's comments, she'd decided to give the bar a try.

There was a bit of a breeze that evening, and she'd tugged her short jacket around her as she approached the black-bricked building. A wrought iron sign above the doorway creaked in the wind, and Ris squinted, attempting to make out the curious creature depicted. Before she could, the door pushed open, a tall orc on a cell phone exited the bar. As the door slowly swung shut, she was able to hear raucous laughter and music spilling from inside, and she reached out quickly, catching the handle and squaring her shoulders before stepping inside.

The bar was bursting with orcs. Ris stepped through the doorway with raised eyebrows, surprised by just how many burly green bodies packed into the space. It was the last place in the world she could imagine demure Silva feeling comfortable, and she chuckled in spite of herself.

The pool tables were clearly the center of the action, and she wondered if anyone would even notice her presence as she moved

to the tall bar. It was not hard to see that wagers were being placed, money changing hands for sport, with a ring of loud, laughing spectators. She walked past two clusters of women, other sightseers, attempting to woo the few orcs who were not thoroughly absorbed by the noisy action taking place at the green felted tables.

"What'll it be, lovely?"

The orc behind the bar had at least a dozen heavy silver rings in his long ears, the weight of which dragged them towards his neck. Bands of copper adorned his left tusk, while the right had been broken off just above the first shiny circlet and filed smooth. He looked a good bit older than the other in the room, and Ris beamed up at his endearment.

"Ginblossom and tonic with rosemary, if you've got it, and a shot of Lysträe."

That had been nearly ten minutes ago. She realized as she sipped her drink, taking another peek at her punkish watcher, smiling at his cocky grin, that she'd not been asked for payment. "Excuse me...did someone pay for my drinks?"

"Aye." The old orc didn't bother looking up from where he wiped down the polished surface of the bar, and Ris pursed her painted lips.

"Am I allowed to know who?"

"Guess that's part o' the game, lovely...the findin' out."

♥♥♥

Silva checked her lipstick in the car's rearview mirror and took a deep breath, attempting to calm her rapid pulse. *It's fine. It's no big deal and it'll be fine...just calm down.* The valet stand was just ahead, car doors opening for sylph-like women in short dresses, dryads and gorgons and nymphs, glamorous and sleek. Just two more cars and then she'd be walking in.

She tried to listen to her inner voice, tried to heed its wise words...but it was wrong. It was wrong, because it *was* a big deal. It was the first time she'd be meeting her boyfriend's friends, the first time he'd ever invited her to do so. It was a *huge* deal. *Not your boyfriend*, she corrected. That wasn't the kind of mistake she could afford to be making, not tonight. She didn't know how to define her relationship with Tate, didn't know what was an acceptable title to call him, but he was not, as the little voice in her head so often reminded her, her boyfriend.

You've been marked, precious one, but I can't tell by whom...the fae woman's words seemed to echo in her bones during the week, nights spent alone in her bed in her small apartment. She didn't know how he would introduce her to these mystery friends, and she didn't want to admit how worried she was over that moment, over what he would call her as aloof eyes flicked in her direction, silently judging. Tate's friends would be as effortlessly cool as he was, she was sure of it—detached and smirking, graceful and poised. Growing up in the country club world of Elvish society meant she was well versed in haughtiness and icy smiles, and Silva was confident she'd be able to hold her own with these people...provided she made it past those fraught introductions.

If she was labeled as *my friend Silva*, she would start to cry. She knew herself well enough to recognize that. Knew that disappointment and despair would mix and bubble and overflow, as if her emotions were some ill-fated science experiment; that she'd have a short window in which to push away from him, to escape to a restroom and have her breakdown in private, and that would be the end.

No more carefree weekend nights spent at the Pixie, perched on a high stool while he tended bar on Rukh's night off, pressing her face to his strong back once the final patron staggered out the door at closing time, slipping her arms around him; no more waking up on Sunday mornings securely pressed against him, no more soft kisses in the grey morning light and lazy lovemaking, no more freedom and mischief and laughter. No coming back.

Stop it! You're not going to do that, it'll be fine. Just follow his lead.

The valet gave her a bright smile as she stepped from the car with her heart in her mouth. The club was sleek and upscale, would be full of the sorts of people she'd gone to school with, a complete one-eighty from Tate's own bar. A minotaur in a tight black shirt stood at the entrance, giving her an appraising once-over as she approached, opening the door before she could even mention that she was with a private party.

Here goes nothing...you can do this. It'll be fine.

♥♥♥

If you enjoyed Girls Weekend, you'll love reading more about the girls hometown of Cambric Creek! Where the neighbors are a little unconventional and the full moon affects more than just the night sky. Sexy werewolves, adorable mothmen, and randy minotaurs welcome you to settle in and make yourself at home! Are you tired of the typical, run-of-the-mill romances featuring the boring Chad next door? Are you longing for a bit of fang and claw in your love story (and maybe a few tentacles for good measure?) Do non-human/human love stories with a scorching heat level and a lot of heart get your pulse pumping?

If so, then set a trap for love with Monster Bait!

♥♥♥

From **Sweet Berries**, *a Monster Bait romance, coming soon:*

"I don't bite, you know." Grace tried to keep her voice light, despite the way she twisted at his sudden distance, a sharp departure from the easy intimacy they'd shared at the observatory.

"Neither do I," came his soft reply, somewhat sadly. His hands, long and graceful, which had reached out to her gently all evening, were clutched tightly in his lap, his eyes trained on the floor.

I don't want you to be afraid of me. Cold prickled her skin at

the thought of the words he'd said at the tree line, at his automatic assumption that he was the cause for her hesitation in the dark. "I'm not." Red eyes met hers in confusion, and she realized she had voiced her response to his unspoken statement aloud. "I'm not afraid of you," she murmured, sliding over the smooth leather to close the distance between their bodies. "I don't know why you'd think that." Wrapping an arm around his as she spoke, Grace leaned against his side and to her immense relief, he didn't pull away.

"Well...that's good. I-I'm glad to hear it." Several moments of silence passed before he spoke again. "The humans I work with...a lot of them tend to keep to themselves, they stick together. And I get it, I'm not a member of their team, they haven't known me for years the way they know each other, it's not the same...but there's always a separation there."

"I'm the first to admit I didn't know a ton about the different cultures before I moved here," she admitted. "And I still don't know about some, but there's only one way you learn, right? The whole 'stick to your species' thing—that's my grandparent's generation."

"It doesn't bother you then?"

Tipping her head back, she considered his profile. His jaw was long, his cheekbones high, his eyes wide and expressive. His shoulders were broad and his chest solid, and she'd already felt the steel-like strength in his leanly-muscled arms. His smoky, violet and gray coloring was ethereal and beautiful, and she couldn't wait to bury her face against the thick mantle of fluff around his neck. He'd be attractive in any species, Grace considered. "Not one bit. You're going to force me to say 'not all humans', aren't you?"

His laughter was deep and rich, vibrating against her in a purr, antennae dancing. "Gods, I hope not!"

Her laughter joined his, and the implication of his words made heat pool low in her belly.

"So does that mean you've never dated a human before?" *Never been with a human...*

"No, I haven't." He clicked and shook out his mantle, avoiding her eye. "I hope I'm not doing everything wrong."

The air outside was balmy and warm, despite the slight breeze at the top of the tree, a perfect summer night, although she suspected that had little to do with the heat that filled her as his long arm slipped around her back. "I had a great time yesterday, and tonight has been wonderful so far, so I think you're doing okay."

"Ah," he began in a low rumble that made her toes curl, "but the night is young." Merrick's wide hand spread out over the side of her hip as his head lowered and Grace felt her heart climb into her throat in excitement over the kiss she knew was coming. "There's plenty

of time for me to screw something up." His thin mouth was warm, and the thumb that pressed circles into her hips was rhythmic in its movement. The flitting movement of the little hummingbirds came to mind as she traced the shape of his lips with the tip of her tongue, and when she pressed into the hot cavern of his mouth, he purred against her, his twilight-colored wings vibrating in a frenzy.

♥♥♥

*Please visit **cmnascosta.com** and follow along on social media, where you can read stories for free, become a patron, and get email alerts for all upcoming publications!*

C.M. Nascosta is an author and professional procrastinator from Cleveland, Ohio. As a child, she thought that living on Lake Erie meant one was eerie by nature, and her corresponding love of all things strange and unusual started young. She's always preferred beasts to boys, the macabre to the milquetoast, the unknown darkness in the shadows to the boy next door. She lives in a crumbling old Victorian with a scaredy-cat dachshund, where she writes nontraditional romances featuring beastly boys with equal parts heart and heat, and is waiting for the Hallmark Channel to get with the program and start a paranormal lovers series. Follow her on social media, and come say hello!

Girls Weekend

Printed in the USA
CPSIA information can be obtained
at www.ICGtesting.com
LVHW031910060923
757435LV00025B/430